A Dopeboy's Dream 3

Lock Down Publications and Ca$h
Presents

A Dopeboy's Dream 3

A Novel by *Romell Tukes*

A Dopeboy's Dream 3

Lock Down Publications
P.O. Box 944
Stockbridge, Ga 30281
www.lockdownpublications.com

Copyright 2021 Romell Tukes
A Dopeboy's Dream 3

Lock Down Publications
Like our page on Facebook: Lock Down Publications @
www.facebook.com/lockdownpublications.ldp

Book interior design by: **Shawn Walker**
Edited by: **Jill Alicea**

Stay Connected with Us!

Text **LOCKDOWN** to 22828 to stay up-to-date with new releases, sneak peaks, contests and more…

Thank you!

Submission Guideline.

Submit the first three chapters of your completed manuscript to ldpsubmissions@gmail.com, subject line: Your book's title. The manuscript must be in a .doc file and sent as an attachment. Document should be in Times New Roman, double spaced and in size 12 font. Also, provide your synopsis and full contact information. If sending multiple submissions, they must each be in a separate email.

Have a story but no way to send it electronically? You can still submit to LDP/Ca$h Presents. Send in the first three chapters, written or typed, of your completed manuscript to:

LDP: Submissions Dept
P.O. Box 944
Stockbridge, Ga 30281

DO NOT send original manuscript. Must be a duplicate.

Provide your synopsis and a cover letter containing your full contact information.

Thanks for considering LDP and Ca$h Presents.

Romell Tukes

Prologue
One Year Prior

Don's name was starting to buzz heavily around the city of Bad News and other cities in VA.

Don and his crew were locking down the streets with the best dog food the city was getting. With money came problems, and Melly was lurking for blood after his role model and mentor Big Bio was killed years ago by the crew.

Homo also was out to kill Don and everything he loved. Homo got close to Don's little brother, 50, and took him under his wing. That relationship didn't last long because 50 robbed Homo for eighty keys so he could build his own empire like his brother. 50 and his best friend, Tank Brim, started to flood the hood with work and word got back to Homo. With so much beef Homo had going on with Don, he had to add 50 to the hit list as well.

Roc and his brother, Twin, were going back and forth with Lil' PJ, Pookie, and Capo. After bumping heads with Ja and Racks, Capo got the drop on Racks, who was an undercover homothug, bisexual. He killed him, leaving Ja alone in the streets. Ja called a sit down with Twin and Roc so they could team up to go at Don's crew and 50.

Don ended up getting locked up for a gun charge weeks after his father, Rich, tried to put him on a plug, who was an FBI agent. Rich was trying to set Don up so he could get outta jail but was unaware the agent was a dirty cop, selling Don his own keys before he started the case.

Luckily, Don got wind that the plug was an agent from Cap. Cole, who was on his payroll. Don killed Turky, the undercover agent, on a boat fishing trip.

When Don landed in Sux 2 Prison, he built a strong bond with his celly, Knight, who was from New York. Don saved his life when prisoners tried to stab him to death, so they had a good bond.

The day Don murdered his pops in the shower, he gave Knight the knife to get rid of, and he did just that.

While in the box, Don was stressed, fighting a body on a two-year sentence. An old head named Ice, who was serving a life sentence, took the murder charge for Don so he could go home.

Don came home in the middle of a crazy war. Pookie, his little homie, got locked up for two murders and for killing a cop. Pookie's father, Pastor Ryan, killed Ja's family and Ja at his place of work. The feds raided Pastor Ryan's church and had a big shoot out. Pastor Ryan went out shooting, as if he was still in the special ops forces overseas when he was serving his country.

50's girlfriend was pregnant, and his mom finally introduced him to his grandfather, whom he never had a bond or relationship with. When 50 saw who his grandfather was, he was sick to see Cap Cole sitting there.

His mom tried to tell 50 that the dirtiest cop in Bad News was his grandpop, so 50 walked out the restaurant, not looking back.

Homo caught up with 50 one night and had him cornered with a gun to his head. The unthinkable happened. Someone shot and killed Homo in front of 50, saving his life. 50 saw his brother, Don, approach outta nowhere. 50 had salty feelings toward Don because he killed their other brother, K.

The same night, they got a call from their mom, who was surrounded at gunpoint in her home by Bloody, who was Rich's son from New York. Bloody killed their mom and went back to New York, promising to be back in days. Keeping his word, Bloody came back and built himself a little crew, ready for war.

Chapter 1
Bad News, VA

Lil' PJ tossed his girlfriend, Stacia, on their California king-sized bed, staring at her sexy body, especially her freshly shaved kitty.

"I been a bad girl," Stacia spoke with a seductive voice while sliding a finger into her drenched pussy.

"Damn, you know what we do to bad girls around here," Lil' PJ stated, role playing with her.

Lil' PJ started kissing on her inner thighs, then made his way to her love box. Stacia moaned while his tongue made contact with her thin pussy lips, as her pussy throbbed for his loving.

"Keep licking right there!" she screamed.

He lowered his lips into the bottom of her pussy and sucked the juices out of her wetness. The way he put the attack game down on her pussy was the main reason why she fell in love with him the first night.

Stacia was a beautiful, chocolate, mocha-complexioned woman with short natural hair, a small waist, and a nice ass. They met a couple of months back at her job in a dental office and since then, it's been a romantic getaway. She knew what type of lifestyle he was into, and she settled for it because she loved him.

"Ohh, shit, baby, stop, stop, I have to go to work. Fuck, I'm late." Stacia pushed him off her and rushed to get dressed.

Lil' PJ was pissed as he laid there horny. He knew he was gonna have to watch Pornhub and get his own rocks off.

"That's fucked up, baby. You knew you had to go to work before I ate your stank ass pussy. That's why you told me to eat it!" he shouted, upset on the low.

"Boy, shut up, now you know how it feels when you be up in this ocean for two minutes, leaving me hanging." She laughed while getting dressed.

"Whatever. I'll see you when you get off, baby, love you," he told her.

"Love you more, ugly." She left him in the crib.

Lil' PJ had to get up with Don in two hours in Dale City to talk about their next shipment. Since Don came home from prison, he controlled the drug operation like he did before he went in. While he was gone, Lil' PJ took over and it was too much for him to handle, especially with all the beef they had going on all over the city.

Beefing with Homo, Melly, Ja, Racks, Rock, and Twin, plus CL was like going against a whole city itself, but luckily, he and his guys were able to come out on top.

Lil' PJ wrote and sent Pookie money every week to make sure he was good in his prison in Greenville, where the DC sniper was also housed. He was sick when his friend blew trial to eight life sentences.

Lil' PJ grabbed his iPad and looked for some old Pinky films so he could masturbate. She was always his go-to girl since he was a kid.

***

Woodbridge, VA

Twin had a young nigga tied up in his storage room in a U-Haul warehouse. His cousin worked up front, so she let him do as he pleased, but only if he paid like he weighed.

"You work for Don, but you never saw him or spoke to him?" Twin asked a young nigga they called Led, who worked for Don.

10

Led ran a small crew in Woodbridge who sold dog food for Don. The past year, Led made probably over two million dollars thanks to Don. The truth was, Led re-upped from Don twice a month in person, but he had loyalty for Don and he wasn't a snake.

"Bruh, I swear I don't even know that nigga! Never saw him or spoke to him!" Led shouted.

"Ok. Yo, Jig, pass me this fuck nigga's phone, dawg," Twin told one of his blood homies.

"Nigga, you got Don's name in your call log, you dumb bitch!" Twin kicked him in his stomach then pulled out his pistol.

Bloc!
Bloc!
Bloc!
Bloc!
Bloc!
Bloc!

The shots echoed through the room, but the storage rooms were all soundproof, so they had nothing to worry about. When Twin saw blood leaking out of Led's head, he told his two personal security guards to bag Led's body up and get rid of it.

Twin had been laying low until recently. He had a small crew of Bloods getting money in Richmond, but he hadn't been on the beefing tip. He hadn't been able to sleep since he heard Don was home. He wanted his head, and he wasn't gonna stop until he got it.

Twin's connect, CL, wanted Don dead for his own desires, so they were the perfect team.

Romell Tukes

Chapter 2
Dale City, VA

Don was leaving his 17,417-sq. ft. mansion in an upper-class neighborhood made for the rich and wealthy. There were three luxury cars in the driveway. He picked the Bentley SUV for today.

He was on his way to meet a young marketing salesman so he could get into investing money in selling car parts. Don was trying to clean up his money because it was coming in so fast, he couldn't keep up with it.

Bad News was filled with the dog food he was pushing out there. Lil' PJ and Capo were out in the streets moving the bricks while Don played the background.

Shit was going as planned for Don and his crew, but Don was on a manhunt for the person who killed his mother. He still didn't have a name, but he knew sooner or later everything would come to light.

Burying his mother was the worst feeling he ever felt in his life. Worse than having to kill his brother, K, even though Bree finished the job.

His little brother, 50, was sick, but they mourned together and came together as a team. 50 was now dealing with Don on the work tip, so he was getting his bricks for basically nothing.

Don had a plug in from DC, but she lived in Miami, so he only met her twice and she was crazy, but Stephen played fair. He had one main focus since last year, and that was to find out who killed his mother.

When 50 told him Cap. Cole was their grandfather, Don thought that was a joke, but 50 told him about the encounter. It didn't make any sense to Don. If Cap. Cole knew they were his grandkids, why would he try to extort them? That was fucked up to him.

The Bentley SUV slid down the city streets, catching attention as always while driving to his destination.

***

Stafford, VA

Capo bopped his head to the loud music playing from the car stereo system parked on the back side of the basketball court. There were thirty goons outside with him enjoying one of the hottest days of the summer. Capo was in his tank top with his diamond necklace hanging from his neck as his pants sagged. They were throwing a barbecue in the back of the projects for Big Chris, who was killed a few years ago by police in the projects.

"Yo, Capo, I'm heading across town to drop that shit off to Seann and them niggas, bruh," one of Capo's runners told him, with a small bookbag on his back on a dirt bike, which was his thing.

"You got two keys for him, right?" Capo asked, putting his cup of lean down on the trunk of an old-school Chevy sitting on big rims with a mean candy apple paint job. The car belonged to one of his workers.

"Yeah."

"Don't give that fat ass nigga shit until he pays you twenty-two thousand from the last shit I gave him, dawg." Capo was serious about his paper.

"I got you." The young boy cranked up the loud dirt bike and left while Capo picked up his cup and rejoined the little party in his hood. Capo was hood rich, but he was still in the hood all day every day. He had a nice two-story house on the outskirts of Stafford.

Things had been real quiet on the beef tip lately since Homo, Ja, Racks, and Roc were all dead, but Capo knew a new wave of drama would be coming soon, especially since Don's mother was kidnapped.

Melly and CL had been M.I.A. and out of the picture for a while now, but Capo thought it was CL that killed his mom, but that was only his personal thought. Capo went to get some more lean and loud to smoke. He was going to hit up some hoes and tell them to come through for his homies.

***

Bad News, VA

50 and three of his goons were in the trap sweating bullets while cutting the heroin with all types of other drugs and pills to give the fiends what they wanted. A good hit. They were in a fiend's house, and the fiend was in the corner on the floor nodding off with the needle still in his arm, making everybody laugh.

"Turn on the AC, yo!" 50 shouted.

"This shit broke, dawg," one of his goons yelled back while bagging up the brownish powder into small, clear paper baggies.

"I know this nigga got a fan." 50 got up from the kitchen table to go find a fan.

The crew was cutting and bagging up ten keys of dope. It was the last of 50's stash until tomorrow, when he went to meet Don in Dale City.

Bad News was half of 50 and his crew. They were doing big things and every drug dealer was copping from either him or Tank Brim. Luckily, 50 ain't have to kill a nigga in months. He was focused on money and getting rich. He was still praying to find the person who killed his mother. He thought about her every night. Ashley's death sent him to a dark place because he was a mama's boy. If Don wasn't there being supportive, he would've gone crazy.

Being in business with Don was so sweet because he was getting 200 to 300 keys at a time on the arm. He finished bagging up the rest of his work and went to Richmond to fuck with his boy, Gem, who was moving work for him out there.

Chapter 3
Washington, DC.

Today was Bloody's twenty-third birthday, and he was in the famous strip club called Station. His VIP section was filled with a bunch of wild DC niggas with dreads ready to kill at his will. Bloody was drinking D'ussé out the bottle, while a gang of women were on the floor twerking and moving their thongs to the side, giving everybody a sneak peek.

DC had been Bloody's location for the last six months. He knew a couple of getting-money niggas from the Southeast section, so he was locking down the drug trade over there with his crew. He had a crew of killers, so nobody thought twice about doing anything to him. A lot of DC cats disliked New York niggas because a big-time gangsta from New York came down to D.C. and told on a lot of good men...legends. After killing Don's mom last year, he went back to New York and moved to DC.

Bloody's father was Rich. He didn't know him too much, but he did know his mom and grandparents hated him for some reason, but nobody ever told him. In Bloody's eyes, his dad was a stand-up, boss-type nigga before Don killed him. Hearing Don was his brother after he got word that Rich's own son killed him, he was confused.

Bloody had a couple of niggas in VA he fucked with heavy, so they put him on game about Don. With an uncle and grandfather as his connect, he couldn't go wrong at all. Bloody had a regular life in the hood. He was from Brooklyn where he ran the streets and became a 9trey blood member. His real name was Brandon, and he was light skinned with long braids, slim, and tall with bushy eyebrows. He also had a scar on his face.

"What's up, daddy?" a slim brown dancer asked Bloody, sitting in his lap.

"You tell me, ma."

"I'm trying whatever you want," she replied, boldly looking back at him. Bloody caught the sign.

"Yo, let me get a minute," he told everybody in the VIP section as twelve people left. Bloody whipped out his dick, and her face said it all.

"Damn, I hope you tipping me, nigga." She got on her knees and wrapped her lips around the tip of his dick, slowly sucking.

The stripper started to go crazy on his rod. Deep throating him, sucking on his balls, and looking him in his eyes. Bloody couldn't take it any more, and she made him cum in her warm mouth. She swallowed everything like a pornstar.

"You taste good." She stood up, extending her hand to get paid. Bloody handed her two thousand dollars.

"Wow." She looked at him because a blow job was normally five hundred dollars.

"Who is them niggas over there?" Bloody saw another crew tossing lots of money all night, and they had his attention. He loved to network.

"Them niggas be coming twice a month. They from VA, but fuck them. I'm trying to go home with you." She smiled, wanting to feel him inside of her because she was horny.

"What the fuck I look like, Captain Save a Hoe? Get the fuck out my section!" Bloody kicked her out and made his way to the other section with his crew.

Bloody approached the men respectfully, and they invited him and his crew to sit down. He and the leader of the pack talked for a good hour. They made plans to link up and everything. When Bloody asked the man about a nigga named Don, he told Bloody he heard of him, but never saw him. Normally, he didn't get too friendly or run his mouth too much, but he was drunk.

"I killed that fuck nigga's mom. He supposed to be my brother, but when I see that Don nigga, it's on sight. I'ma need a few good men like you and your crew just in case, and I got on the best dog food and coke fresh from New York, son," Bloody whispered into the man's ear, almost covering it with his spit.

"I got you," the man stated.

"I hope so. I plan on opening up shop in VA next month." Bloody took a sip of liquor.

"Oh yeah, bruh? Where at?"

"Bad News, you heard…"

"It's a little crazy out there. How you going to take over if you don't know nobody?" the man asked.

"I got a couple of blood homies out there, but my main goal is to take over all of Don's traps and then kill him slow, facts. Word is bond." Bloody's voice deepened.

"I'm with you, just call me when you done, but me and my crew gotta get up outta here." The man embraced Bloody after exchanging numbers. Once the man who was talking to Bloody left the club, he pulled out his phone.

"Yo, Don, what's up, this Capo. We need to talk right now…"

Romell Tukes

Chapter 4
Dale City, VA
Hours Later

Don woke up out of his sleep to get the doorbell for Capo, who recently called him talking about it being an emergency. He walked downstairs in his Versace pajamas and slippers.

"Hold the fuck up, bruh," Don shouted while Capo kept ringing the bell like he didn't see Don walking downstairs.

"What's taking you so long?" Capo said as he busted through the doors. Don was about to tell him about himself, but it was too late to argue with him.

"Capo, chill the fuck out. Now what happened?" Don followed him into his kitchen.

"I was in DC at the Station, doing me with a couple niggas from around da way, you feel me. Some New York nigga came over to my section with some DC cats." Capo paused when he saw the crazy look on Don's face, because he thought the same thing. Seeing a New York dude in DC was rare, because the two states disliked each other from past events.

"That's odd," Don said to himself.

"Let me finish, dawg, you always want to cut me off. So, the dude's name is Bloody and he from Brooklyn. He started telling me how he the plug and how he got DC on lock, and he had some people in Bad News." When Capo explained a story, he went on and on like he was in a movie.

"Get to the point."

"Aight, peep game. He gets to telling me how he killed a chick named Ashley, your mom. He said a nigga named Don killed his dad, Rich, and you was supposed to be his brother or some shit. He also asked if I knew you, I said no, but I think this is ole buddy we been looking for," Capo said, taking a deep breath.

Don was silent. He'd never heard of Bloody, or Rich having another son, but he wouldn't put it past him.

"What else he say?"

"He coming to Bad News and he trying to network, so we exchanged phone numbers. I should've killed that nigga right there, but I had to think it out," Capo told Don, who was in deep thought.

"Nah, bruh, you did good. We just gonna wait, but I want you to find out who in the city he fucking with."

"I can do that. I got a feeling this nigga gonna be a big problem," Capo repeated.

"What's new? I'm going back to sleep, dawg. Lock the door when you leave." Don went upstairs to get some rest. Hearing he found his mom's killer was the best news he heard all year, but the bad news was, he didn't know who he was up against.

***

Richmond, VA
FBI Headquarters

Agent Brooke was the prettiest black woman in the FBI building. At the age of thirty, she had her life together and she was focused. She was raised in Bad News, but when she went to college at Georgetown University, she never looked back.

Brooke had been in the FBI for eight years now. She had a good, strong resume and was respected among the men in the building, which was rare. She used to live with her boyfriend, Mell, who was into real estate. The two met sixteen months ago, but they were deep in love. At first, she thought they were moving too fast, but Brooke knew love didn't have a speed limit. Until he started to cheat, and she kicked him out. Her family still lived in Bad News, but their relationship wasn't good, especially with her brother, Jeezy, who was deep in the streets gangbanging and selling dope.

Yesterday, she got a new case on her desk that was in Bad News. She was shocked and overwhelmed to see all the murders and drug dealing taking place. One thing she did see was the last agent, Turky, who tried to solve the case and go undercover, came up dead in a river. Brooke wasn't going undercover. She almost lost her life twice doing that in two big cases. There were so many people on her report she didn't know who was who. The main people she was about to have her brown eyes on were Don, CL, Capo, Lil' PJ, and Melly.

***

Greensville Prison, VA

Pookie warmed up a soup in his sink, hitting the bag with the hot water. He only got to come out of his cell an hour a day. This was a twenty-three-and-one-hour lockdown prison.

Seeing other inmates was rare, but Pookie had plans to transfer to a better jail in a couple of months.

This was his new life, so he was used to it already, but he wished he could hurry up and die. Hearing the news of him having HIV last year crushed him, but he learned to live with it. He didn't even want to take medication. He was just counting his days. Luckily, his boys, Lil' PJ, Don, and Capo, held him down and kept him alive in spirit, because it was hard knowing he was never coming home.

Romell Tukes

Chapter 5
Richmond, VA

Bloody puffed on a blunt of loud he got from Cali last week. He smoked by the pound, that was his thing, getting high. He sat in the backseat of the SUV while his goons drove him to the airport to meet CL.

Since Bloody had been in the DMV area, he'd been hearing CL's name when niggas mentioned VA. When it came to DC, a chick named Stephen ran the drug game, and word was she was a bad bitch, but crazy. Bloody tried to reach out to Stephen, but he got no reply, so he left it at that and continued to do his thing.

When he had his VA niggas reach out to CL, he accepted and told Bloody to meet him at his private jet. The only thing on Bloody's mind was networking and taking over VA in a matter of months.

CL looked out the window of his private jet, waiting for his guest, who was a half an hour late for their meeting. He recently changed his name in the streets to "The King of VA," and he was standing on that.

Today he wore a suit and tie because he was going to Vegas for the weekend and he planned to take Bloody with him. There were six big, buff security guards standing in the back. The jet was huge with two bedrooms, two bathrooms, sixteen seats, and installed laptops in the wall. Looking at his Richard Muller watch, he planned to give Bloody two more minutes before he told the pilot to pull off.

Business was good and CL was moving heavy weight in VA, West VA, Atlanta, Maryland, and Philly. The past year dealing with Don and his crew was a headache, so he had to boss up and network. Now he was seeing millions by the week, or at least half of that. When he saw the SUV pull up outside, he knew who it was, and he was relieved because he was about to leave.

Bloody stepped on the flight with his goons, to see CL sitting with an upset face as if he was pissed off.

"What's up, fam?" Bloody had his New York swag on full blast. VA niggas weren't too heavy on New York cats because they always came down to VA and tried to take over, and CL was against it.

"Sit down." CL looked him up and down, wondering what could a nigga like Bloody have to talk to him about. CL did his research on Bloody and the kid was stamped in DC as an official nigga, but CL liked to feel niggas out himself.

"My bad I'm late, I'm coming from DC" Bloody sat across from CL, not feeling his vibes at all.

"I understand." CL felt the jet take off.

"I'm Bloody. Thanks for meeting me."

"I know who the fuck you are. Tell your men to go to the back with my goons." CL nodded at his goons and Bloody did the same. Once the guards all went in the back, the men started talking.

"I heard a lot about you, and I respect your grind, bro."

"Enough of the ass kissing. What do you want?" CL was straightforward.

"I'm trying to network. I'm the plug and I got them keys for dirt cheap, and I know we can do some big things together, son," Bloody said.

"Is that right?"

"Facts! Whatever number you get your shit for, I will go lower with the best product. My plug is amazing and I'm the face to our empire," Bloody said strongly.

"Who's your plug?"

"You don't know him, but his name is Fats. My uncle got New York on lock," Bloody boasted.

"Oh yeah?"

"Trust me, I got you." Bloody knew he had CL by the look on his face.

"Do you know me and my brother been supplying Fats for years?" CL's question threw him so far off he ain't know what to say or do.

"Huh…"

"You heard me. I supply your plug, so I'm acting like we never had this conversation. We're gonna go to Vegas and have a good time, and that's the end of that," CL said with a fake smile, pulling out his laptop to type something.

Bloody felt dumb. He thought he did his research on CL, but he never knew he had a brother or supplied his uncle.

"I ain't know, my bad, bro."

"It's over, but how you give up your plug so fast? I could have been the feds or anybody. You gotta think next time. Never let greed blind your vision and purpose," CL stated as Bloody nodded his head and took a nap.

When Bloody woke up, he was in Vegas. They had a ball there. CL knew how to have a good time and so did Bloody. He was a party animal.

Romell Tukes

Chapter 6
Bad News, VA

Tank Brim and his little cousin, Lil' Two, who was a gay female and dressed as a boy, waited in the car watching the trap house. Lil' Two was a cute chick, but she tried so hard to be a man she didn't have sex appeal. She had a big ass and long hair. If she was to dress up, she would fool anybody.

She just started to chill with Tank Brim since coming back to VA from living in Atlanta. Lil' Two was a blood gang member under Tank Brim, who was now a big homie with a lot of rank in VA.

Growing up, she used to always look up to Tank, even though he was only a couple of years older than her. Their mothers were sisters, but they had a big family in VA and Atlanta. At 18 years old, she was already a known shooter and known for turning up. At first, Tank Brim didn't want her hanging with him, but he would rather her be with him than some nigga who was gonna have her in jail looking sick.

"They must be getting money. Them niggas never leave that spot." Lil' Two watched fiends run in and out the beat-up house to cop drugs.

"Yeah, they been out here for a few weeks. I know they seeing some big money. I just want to know who they work for," Tank Brim said.

"You know I never seen niggas just pop up on niggas' block and move weight. Normally, somebody knows somebody." Lil' Two wasn't a drug dealer, but she knew how the streets worked.

Tank Brim had three trap spots in Bad News that he and 50 opened. Their spots were up the block from where Tank and 50's trap was, so the new niggas on the block were stopping their money.

"Follow my lead…" Tank Brim got out the truck, making his way across the street.

Three young hustlers posted up in the living room counting money, eating pizza, and smoking weed.

Boom!!

The door busted open and two of the young boys grabbed two AK-47s from the floor, but the gunmen didn't give them a chance to fire off any shots.

Boc!!

Boc!!

Boc!!

Boc!!

One of the young niggas caught four to the chest from Lil' Two's gun, and Tank Brim fired two bullets into the other man's head. The man's dead body dropped in the last man standing's lap, scaring him to death.

"Please, bruh, don't kill me," the last nigga stated.

"Who you work for and where can I find him?" Tank Brim asked.

"I work for Bloody, he from New York. I just met him a few weeks ago and he told us to open shop right here. I got a lot of work, dawg. I don't know where he live, but I swear you will never hear from me again," the man cried.

Boc!!

Boc!!

Boc!!

Lil' Two shot him in the face and collected all the money and drugs as Tank Brim just shook his head at her because she didn't listen.

***

Norfolk, VA

In a nice middle-class area, 50 and Jazzy had a nice house with a clean and manicured front yard. Jazzy took the blindfold off 50's eyes as he laid on the king-sized bed, ass naked, ready for their role-play night.

Their daughter was finally asleep in the baby room, so they planned to get freaky tonight. Jazzy wore a schoolgirl's outfit with nothing under it. She turned around and bent over to shake her fat ass, turning him on. 50 saw her bold, fat pussy and couldn't wait to eat her pussy. Jazzy got on the bed and grabbed his dick.

"I love you, daddy," she said before she sucked the tip then swallowed his whole pole, using her full lips to move up and down. 50 thrusted his hips into her face, ramming his dick down her mouth until he unloaded.

"My turn." She climbed on his face and 50 started tongue fucking her soaked pussy, spreading her pussy lips.

"Ahhh, yessss." Jazzy started to grind and bounce on his face as he focused on sucking on the clit. He moved his tongue in circular motions, making her go crazy until she came. Jazzy then rode his dick until she heard the baby crying, blowing her shit and stopping the party.

Romell Tukes

Chapter 7
Stafford, VA

Capo recently made it back to Stafford after his trip to Richmond.

"Bruh and nem ain't picking up the phone. They shit all going to voicemail," Pole said, driving the Lexus on rims through the hood.

"Swing by their spot real quick. Dem clowns got 15 keys over there and they got their phones off? Something ain't right." Capo looked out his window at all the niggas out in the projects standing around bored.

Capo's main focus was trying to figure out what's up with some niggas he heard opening shop in his hood. Tonight, he was going to meet one of his little soldiers, so he could get the inside scoop on what was going on. They pulled up to the project apartment and looked around to see it was a little quiet around the area.

"All these niggas fired, dawg, on some real shit, shawty!" Capo shouted, walking into the apartment through the unlocked front door.

"What the fuck..." Capo said as he walked all the way inside the crib to see dead bodies and blood puddles everywhere.

Capo went searching for the drugs. He didn't find a piece of dog food laying around, leaving him to think someone robbed him of 15 bricks of heroin.

"Fuck, man!" Capo yelled, kicking the living room table, breaking it.

"I know it's them new niggas in town, it gotta be, dawg. Them niggas had the drop on us." Pole made sense because nobody would disrespect Capo like that, especially in his hood.

"Let's slide bruh. We about to get down to the nitty gritty of this shit." Capo walked out the house, ready to kill the whole city until he found out who crossed him.

The man inside the old school hooptie with the tints watched Capo and Pole come out the house, upset with confused looks, making him smile.

Melly watched Capo get in the Lexus and pull off. He waited a few seconds before pulling off to follow him. Melly ran up in Capo's trap and killed all his goons and robbed him for 15 keys he didn't need. The past couple of months, he'd been hiding out in Maryland getting money, but he was also in West Virginia trapping hard with a small cut there.

He was back for revenge to finish what he started, because he knew if he didn't kill Don and his crew, then he would spend the rest of his days in fear. Seeing Capo gave him an erection in his dick. He wanted to kill him right there, but he knew patience was big in the type of situation he was in. One slip could blow his cover, and he wanted to remain under the radar and cause mischief in the land.

He followed the Lexus all around town, studying Capo's every move, so when the time came, he could strike.

***

Dale City, VA

"Thanks for pulling up on me, dawg. I've been trying to holler at you anyway for a few days." Don poured himself a glass of liquor from his living room bar.

"Yeah. What's up though, cuz? Pour me a glass of dat shit, bruh." 50 leaned back in Don's recliner chair.

"Nah, you don't need this, bruh. I need you to stay focused. We got some real shit we about to face, bruh." Don got serious.

"What?"

"I found out who killed Mommy, and we about to enter a big war so, I need you and your crew to be on deck because we don't know who we about to be up against, bruh," Don said, sitting down.

"When you found this shit out?" 50's blood rushed to his head.

"Capo met some nigga at a club in DC bragging about him killing Mommy and how he was looking for me, so I'm gonna do my research."

"Why would he just pop up looking for you?" 50 thought he was leaving something out.

"He's Rich's son from New York. I guess he wants pay-back for Rich or some shit. I don't know, but whatever it is, that shit don't matter now, because our mom is dead."

"What we going to do?" 50 asked, hoping Don had a plan.

"I don't know, but I am figuring it out, bruh, facts. Just stay on point, because we don't know what these niggas on," Don stated seriously.

"Aight." 50 got up and left, pissed off.

Romell Tukes

Chapter 8
Hampton, VA
One Month Later

Bloody had a nice little house in the Hampton area that he shared with his new female friend.

Arie looked alluring in her two-toned slip dress with a slit in both sides, showing a lot of skin, turning her man on. At thirty-three years of age, she looked no older than eighteen because she took care of herself. She was a fitness trainer and worked at a wellness center in Hampton.

When Bloody met her in the gym, it was over. He won her heart on their date. Since then, they moved in together and were happy.

Her skin was a light golden complexion, and she had golden hair, nice perky breasts, a heart-shaped ass, and cute face. She was raised in Maryland, but she moved to VA after attending Virginia Tech University.

"You missed me today?" she said, taking off her heels, showing her pretty toes in their master bedroom.

They'd just come back from a nice dinner date in Richmond.

"That's a fact, ma." Bloody took off his outfit.

"I'm not your ma, I'm your wife," she corrected him.

"You know what I mean. I'ma New York nigga, Arie."

"Yeah, I know. That's why I love you." She saw him coming her way.

"Is that the only reason why you love me?" He was now climbing between her legs, spreading them open slowly, laying her on her back.

"Show me the other reason why I love you, I forgot," she moaned, feeling him slide his finger into her bald, fat coochie.

Bloody pulled his dick out and slowly made his way into her tight and dark tunnel.

"Uhmmmmm, baby, yesss…" she said, loving every time he put his dick in her.

As he got deeper in her waterfall, he picked up the pace and started fucking her wildly.

"Ugh…ugh…oh my god, yessss…" she screamed as his manhood penetrated in and out of her love box, leaving juices all over the place.

Bloody pulled his dick out, teasing her, then rammed himself back into her as his pelvis clapped on her pussy until they both came hard.

"I need a break, daddy, please, my pussy hurt." She got up trying to walk the pain off because he was trying to make her pussy sore.

"Come suck this dick then."

"Can we 69?" she asked.

"Yeah," he said, laying down so she could sit on his face and get her box eaten.

Arie made love to his pole while he ate her out with no remorse. Like a true savage.

She was climaxing back to back. She liked his head game better than his sex game. It took Bloody twenty minutes to bust a nut in her mouth, but she spit it back out on his dick because she disliked the taste of cum. It was yucky.

It didn't take long for both to fall asleep in each other's arms. Bloody had to go to Bad News tomorrow to check on his new trap since Capo shut down his last trap house.

***

Woodbridge, VA

Twin ordered some fries and a double cheese chicken sandwich because he didn't eat beef. While ordering his food, he saw a sexy redbone chick with colorful eyes and a fat ass working in the back. He couldn't keep his eyes off her at all. She was stunning, and he had to have her.

When she saw him eyeing her, she tried to play it off, but the energy was so strong her coworkers felt it. Twin got his food and went to sit down near the window. He was going to leave, but he wanted to see the chick again. There was something about her. He didn't care that she worked at McDonald's, or if she was an Instagram model.

In a couple of days, Twin planned to meet up with CL, but first, he was trying to get the drop on Don and his crew, but they were moving smart this time.

The redbone was walking to the restroom. When she saw Twin, she started blushing hard.

"Hey, shawty, let me holla at you one second."

"What's up?" she replied, chewing on gum.

"Can you sit down? I just need a second of your time, please," he said as she looked at him then took a seat.

Twin talked to the woman for over an hour. Her name was Mesha. She was twenty-one with a son and single. They laughed and enjoyed each other's company. Twin gave her $10,000 and told her to quit her job so he could take care of her and her son.

Mesha thought he was playing, but when she saw he was serious, she was on board and left McDonald's with him.

Romell Tukes

Chapter 9
Richmond, VA

Don and 50 were in the old Impala with tints, following the two gray SUV trucks. The sunny and warm evening made it more of the perfect day to kill someone. The brothers were following CL and his goons to an unknown location.

"I hope we get this nigga, dawg," Don mumbled.

"We will, but what's up with this Bloody fool?" 50 asked.

"I got Lil' PJ and Capo on it, bruh, just be patient."

"I think we should handle this situation ourselves because he ain't kill their mom, he killed ours, you feel me." 50 wanted to put in his own work. He didn't want other niggas to do it because that made a nigga look weak.

"We will, 50, just chill. Everything will come together." Don tailed the trucks into a small park with a basketball court, wondering what CL was doing.

"Why they parking?" 50 grabbed his AR-15 assault rifle, which was a little heavy.

"I don't know, but as soon as the doors open, turn up." Don parked near the trash can, attaching his 30-round clip to his handgun.

They saw both truck doors open, and niggas got out with basketballs and shorts, as if they were about to have a tournament.

Tat!..

Tat!..

Tat!..

Tat!..

Tat!..

50 shot two of CL's goons in the back, then all hell broke loose. Every one of CL's goons were shooting at the Impala,

even CL. Don hit one of CL's goons in his heart and another one in his pelvic area.

CL saw Don and 50 aiming for his head. Trying to save his own life, he jumped in one of the trucks, racing off, leaving his last two men. 50 shot CL's last two gunmen, seeing CL run off in the truck.

"That hoe ass nigga!" 50 shouted, upset, getting back inside the Impala with Don and leaving the failed mission.

***

Richmond, VA

Jeezy blew smoke out of his mouth while coming out of a small project area he was running. He was on his way to Bad News, VA to holler at his homie, Bloody, about some business.

Jeezy had a few blood homies in Bad News, so he was known out there. He'd known Bloody for over ten years when he used to go to New York to visit his family in Brooklyn, where Bloody was from.

At the age of thirty-one, he was focused on money and getting rich. His sister Brooke was an FBI agent, but the two had a strong dislike for each other because of their lifestyles. He had long dreads, was short and heavy set, had gold teeth and brown skin. He had a beautiful girlfriend named Maizy. They'd been together since they were kids.

He climbed in his old school, hooked-up Chevy, sitting on big rims, and made his way to Bad News.

***

Virginia Beach, VA

CL's mind was spinning like crazy as he waited for Twin to show up. He was parked behind a high school waiting for Twin so he could try to get him on his team because he needed a soldier.

A black car pulled up with dark tints and black rims. Twin got out, walking over to CL, and got inside his Bentley.

"What's up? I got your message, fool. What it do?" Twin asked, not shaking his hand or nothing, showing no type of respect.

"Thanks for coming out, but I need you, Twin. I'm not going to sit here and play games with you, big bruh," CL said with no shame.

"The big bad CL needs help. I can't believe this shit, dawg. Who got your thongs stuck in your ass under your tail?" Twin planned to have a good time torturing him because Twin knew he was a pussy. He knew the only thing CL was good for was putting money on niggas' heads, but some niggas' heads were priceless.

CL let his little comments slide and focused on what he called him out there for.

"Don and that kid 50 I been hearing about. I need them dead. I know you beef with Don, so who better than you to help. I'm willing to pay whatever or give you however many bricks you can dream of."

"I'll get back at you, but we have a deal. Just stay alive." Twin hopped out the car and headed back to his car, shaking his head.

Romell Tukes

Chapter 10
Dale City, VA

Don got off at his exit to where he lived. Spending hours with Capo and Lil' PJ was a headache. They wanted to shut the city down and find Twin and this new Bloody nigga.

There was a red light off the exit next to a post office. While he was changing his CD, a van pulled up beside him and opened the side door.

Tat!!
Tat!!
Tat!!
Tat!!
Tat!!

Rounds from the AK-47 caught Don in his left arm, but he was able to put the car in drive. He bent the corner, hitting 80 mph at top speed on his way home. He thought he was hit, but it was only a graze.

Bloody and two of his flunkies rode off in the van, listening to him scream and shout.

"I fucking told you to line up the shot! He wasn't even paying attention, you dumb ass nigga!" Bloody screamed from the back seat.

"My bad, bruh. I thought I hit him in the shoulder," Lil' Ship said from the passenger seat, hoping Bloody would shut the fuck up.

"The shoulder? Nigga, you fucking joking? You grazed him, you bitch nigga!" Bloody yelled, getting heated.

"It won't happen again," Lil' Ship told him, trying to end the conversation.

"Aight, son," Bloody replied calmly.

"Where we going, Bloody?" the driver asked, driving down the road.

"Pull over, I gotta take a piss real quick," Bloody told the driver, who pulled over on the dark side road. When the van stopped, Bloody opened the door.

Tat!!

Tat!!

Tat!!

The bullet landed in the back of Lil' Ship's head, killing him. When the driver saw his boy's head slam into the dashboard, he jumped outta fear.

Bloody snatched Lil' Ship's body out the car and tossed him on the side of the road.

"Drive, nigga," he said nonchalantly, and the driver did as he was told.

***

Hampton, VA

Melly waited on the hood of his car, parked outside of a close car wash. He was supposed to be meeting a potential client here that he met over the phone through a nigga he went to school with. There were five bricks in his trunk and a duffle bag full of guns he was planning to sell to the man.

A Jeep pulled up behind him and shut off the lights. The man that got out was a tall, skinny, funny looking, brown-skinned brother.

"Melly, right?"

"Yeah. You Chance, right?"

"Yep. My people spoke good about you. I'm straightforward. I been moving coke and weapons my whole life. I had a plug, but he ran off with my money," Chance stated.

"Don't worry, you're in good hands, bruh," Melly confirmed, walking back to his trunk. Chance saw Melly pop the trunk and smiled.

"This shit looks like some good coke, how much?"

"For you, $29K a joint," Melly replied.

"Where these special weapons I been hearing about so much?" Chance said as Melly grabbed the bag in the deep back and opened it up. Chance started to name every gun in the bag. Even Melly didn't know none of the guns' names he got from his cousin.

"How you know all that, bruh? You know the serial numbers too?" Melly joked.

"I was in the Navy for ten years. I just came back from overseas two years ago," Chance stated as Melly's face scowled.

Melly pulled out his gun and put it to Chance's forehead.

"Nigga, I look dumb to you?" Melly's face was serious.

"Chill bruh, you trippin'." Chance threw his hands up.

"You say you sell coke, but you here to buy dope. Does this tannish key look like coke, you dumb ass nigga?" Melly pointed at the key.

"I sell both," Chance protested.

"You say you was just in the Navy, but Big T said you just did ten years in prison with him. So, who are you?" Melly asked, seeing the look on his face.

"Look, man. You don't want to do this. I'm telling you, it's bigger than you think."

Bloc!

Bloc!

Bloc!

Bloc!

Melly closed the trunk and left Chance's body there before racing off down the block. He saw police lights behind him racing into the carwash. Melly couldn't believe how fast that was. He knew it was a set up.

Romell Tukes

Chapter 11
Bad News, VA

Stacia posted up at the lobby desk of her job at the dental office, bored to death. She was playing on her new iPhone, watching people post up crazy videos on Instagram. She had a lot of followers but did not care about the attention because she knew she was a bad bitch.

Being in a relationship with Lil' PJ, she tried to keep out of the public eye because she saw social media ruin a lot of her friends' love lives. Lil' PJ was popular in the city of Bad News, and she had a lot of haters out there also that would love to take her spot.

A handsome man walked inside the dental office trying to look like a thug.

"Can I make an appointment to get my teeth cleaned today?" the man said.

"I'm sorry, but I'm the only one here right now. The dentist will be here any minute, and he may be able to squeeze you in," Stacia honestly stated.

"I'll wait."

"You can have a seat over there by the plant." She pointed to the other end of the room.

"Nah, I'm good, I'll do a rain check," the man said.

"Ok, bye," she said, looking back to her phone. She didn't even see the gun pointed at her head until it was too late.

Boom!!

Boom!!

The bullets went through her skull, killing her and leaving her head on the desk.

Twin walked out and ran right into the Indian dentist.

"What was that noise?" the man said, peeking over Twin's shoulder.

Twin fired five bullets into the dentist, then tossed him on the floor before he walked off, on his way to Norfolk.

***

North Bad News, VA

Jeezy's girlfriend Tayshia's water just broke at 10:40 pm. She was expecting a baby boy. If Jeezy wasn't in Richmond, then he was in Bad News opening traps with his 9trey blood homies.

"Come on baby, take your time." Jeezy guided her outside the crib to his car, so he could take her to the hospital.

"Just shut up and get me to the fucking hospital, you fucking cheater," she shot back, because she caught him cheating last week and today, he was texting her sister.

Tayshia was an ugly dark woman with a fat ass and a mean head game that drove niggas crazy.

Driving to the hospital, she was so busy yelling and screaming Jeezy didn't see the black-on-black Impala pull up to the passenger side at a red light.

Boc!!
Boc!!
Boc!!
Boc!!
Boc!!
Boc!!
Boc!!

When the Impala turned the corner, Tayshia had blood pouring out of her stomach and neck. Jeezy was horrified. He couldn't even pull off seeing her dead body. Once he was back in his zone, he drove her to the hospital, but it was worthless. She was dead.

Capo parked the Impala in his man's car lot in the hood and got inside his old school donk with rims. For a week now, he and Don had been doing research on Bloody and found out he was a high-ranking 9 trey blood member, so they knew he would be in tune with other gang members in the same set. It was no way a nigga from outta town would come into another state and city without knowing someone before opening trap houses all around the city.

When they did their research on Jeezy, who was from Richmond but had some pull in Bad News, everything came together. Capo went to his side bitch's crib since she was cooking a big dinner for him.

***

Greenville Prison, VA

Lil' PJ was in the small visit room waiting on Pookie to come out. When he got word about Stacia's death, he went crazy ready to kill whoever, but then he realized it was his fault she was dead. Pookie came out in an orange jumpsuit.

"Damn, bruh, this a surprise," Pookie said, sitting down.

"I had to come see you, dawg, you dig me. How you holding up?"

"I'm reading the Qur'an and hood books all day. We locked in the cell for twenty-three hours, so shit be rough. You see I got a beard. What's up with the guys? I miss everybody." Pookie was serious, he thought about everybody a lot.

"We all good, got some new party animals." Lil' PJ referred to party animals as ops.

"I'm sure they came to the right party," Pookie said as they talked the whole visit about the streets.

Romell Tukes

Chapter 12
Norfolk State University

Chavonne wanted to tap out as Twin slid inside of her tight, wet pussy, gripping her wide waist.

"Ohhhh, yesss, Twin…" she cried out, taking his whole length.

She made her ass cheeks clap together on his dick while her sex walls gripped his pole, applying pressure. Twin was so lost inside of her body he didn't know if he was coming or going.

"Mmmm, shit, girl," Twin whispered, ready to erupt.

Chavonne's coochie juice was all over his cock and pelvis area as he pounded her back out until they both climaxed and went limp. She got in the reverse cowgirl position and rode him fast and furious while french kissing him.

"Aaaghhh, oh my god, fuck me harder," she screamed at the top of her lungs as she felt her orgasm rampaging through her body, ready to explode.

Twin grabbed her waist as he fucked her with no mercy on her dorm room twin-sized bed while her roommate was out at a party on campus. When she came, her juices bust everywhere as she squirted on him, the bed, and the floor.

"Damn, shawty," Twin said when she was done, passing her a towel next to his head.

Twin met Chavonne a few weeks back at a college football game, and they clicked from there. On their fourth date, Chavonne couldn't take it anymore. She loved Twin's thuggish swag and attitude. She took him back to her dorm and started sucking his dick as she did in her dreams.

She was twenty years old and in college for computer software technology. She was a mixed breed of Haitian and

Colombian. Her tannish skin, fat ass, and cute face drove men overboard for her attention.

"I think I'm in love with you," she said, trying to gather her thoughts after her crazy sex adventure.

"That sounds like pillow talk to me, shawty." Twin got dressed, ready to head back to Bad News to see if Lil' Two was ready for her mission.

"What I'm speaking is from my heart," she replied, putting on her nightgown, about to change her bed sheets.

"Ok, well, time will tell, love, but I have to go."

"Oh, so now I'm just a hoe. You fuck the shit outta me and leave." She was upset now.

"Chill, shawty. I'm coming back next weekend."

"You sure?" she shot back with puppy dog eyes.

"Yes. I need that little fat pussy in my life." Twin made her smile when he said that.

Twin left and made his way back to Bad News. He called Lil' Two, but her phone was off. He told her the plans days ago for tonight. He didn't know why her phone was off. He was starting to get frustrated with her stubborn ass.

***

Bad News, VA

Lil' Two blew weed smoke out of her nose, trying not to choke. Lil' Wayne played in her stereo as she bobbed her head to music, waiting for 50 to come out of the project building he had just gone in with two people.

She turned off her phone so Twin wouldn't call her. Lil' Two didn't like when he would treat her like a kid. Being a female in the field was hard enough because niggas didn't take women as serious killers. Her goal was to change niggas' thought process about women, so she chose to come on this mission without him. Twin found out 50 and Tank Brim had a trap spot in this area, so they made plans to get at them here.

50 picked up $370,000 and dropped off seventeen keys to his workers, Will and Zack, who were selling keys at a rapid pace.

"I gotta go, but I'll come through in a couple days," 50 said before leaving behind his two young boys he just hired, showing them the ropes.

Outside, nobody saw the masked gunman step out from behind the tree.

Tat!!

Tat!!

Tat!!

The bullets hit one of 50's men, knocking him down, while the other one ran off, leaving 50 alone. Without hesitation, 50 pulled out his handgun and aimed at the shooter who had an AK assault rifle.

Boc!!

Boc!!

Boc!!

Lil' Two got shot in the hand, making her cry out in pain as she was now unable to shoot back. She went back to the car, driving off, ducking 50's bullets.

50 heard a female's voice when he shot and was at a loss for words and confused. He'd never seen that before.

Romell Tukes

Chapter 13
Bad News, VA

BK, whose real name was Kirk Restly, opened a bike store in Bad News. The store had bicycles, dirt bikes, motorcycles, four wheelers, T-rex's and scooters. He also opened a tire store in Richmond, all within four months of being in Virginia.

BK was from Brooklyn. He was every woman's dream, sexy and chocolate with shit going on for himself. His life looked like peaches and cream, but it wasn't at all. He'd been through a lot in his twenty-eight years on earth. Both of his parents were crackheads, so he and his sister raised themselves in the streets.

Growing up in New York, it was either you hustled or starved, and BK wasn't about to fall victim, so he hustled. Once he met a plug on the coke, his life changed, and he started getting money in the Brooklyn streets.

Last year, the feds took down his crew, but luckily, BK played the background and never showed his face while he let his sister run the business aspect of things. Now his sister was sitting in a women's federal prison with five life sentences because she didn't tell on him. He made sure he paid for all her lawyer fees and he made sure she was good in prison, not wanting for shit.

When that federal raid happened, BK laid low and made plans to relocate, and since he had family in VA, a new setting was perfect for him. His cousins were in the dope game in Bad News, Hampton, and Norfolk, which made him want to get back in the game. One of his cousins told him about a nigga named CL, who had the city on lock and the dope for a low price. BK told his cousin to set up a meeting because the dope game was calling him since he touched down in VA. Even though he was a couple of millions up, he needed more.

***
Hampton, VA

Melly had been laying low lately after he saw his face all over the news for killing a federal agent at a car wash. He was now on the FBI Most Wanted list already. Melly knew something was off about the man, but he trusted his people, only to be crossed.

Today he planned to go to DC, then take a flight to Texas, where his uncle lived. His uncle knew he was coming, so Melly was in a rush, but his car had no gas in it. He saw a gas station ahead, so he made a left at the stop sign.

Don and his crew were the last thing on his mind right now. He really cursed himself for coming back to VA. If it wasn't for Don, he wouldn't be in this bullshit. Getting out of the car, he realized the gas area was packed, so he went in the store to pay for gas ahead of time and to grab some snacks. It was 10 am and he thought it was a good idea to get outta town early, so he could see everything around him.

Waiting in the line inside the store, two men and a woman were getting impatient while the store clerk moved at a snail's pace. The clerk was upset he was doing overtime today, so he wanted to make everybody else's day hell too. When it was Melly's turn, he paid for gas and his snacks, paying the man's bad attitude no mind. Outside, a gas pump was empty, so he pulled his car up to the station. He wore a hoodie in 90-degree heat. While pumping gas, Melly felt cold steel pressed to his head.

"Don't fucking move, you're under arrest," the voice said from behind him.

Melly quickly elbowed the man in his stomach and took off running, but he didn't know the off-duty cop used to be a college running back for LSU. The off-duty cop was in the store buying some beers when he saw Melly walk in with a hoodie on. The cop found it weird that a man would have on a hoodie in the hot summer heat. When he saw a good shot of Melly's face in the light, he recognized him from the news for the FBI agent killed. He called it in and took it upon himself to approach the man they claimed to be armed and dangerous. It didn't take long for the cop to tackle Melly and place him in cuffs while six police pulled up to help arrest him.

Melly was charged with murdering a federal agent after the police beat the shit out of him twice at the police station. They claimed he was resisting arrest with cuffs on, so they whipped his ass. He was hauled off to Arlington County Jail the next day with two black eyes and a busted lip and nose.

Romell Tukes

Chapter 14
Bad News, VA

Jeezy saw Bloody get out of his truck with an exhausted look on his face. The two had known each other for years, so Jeezy knew when something was off with his blood homie.

"What's poppin', Bloody." Jeezy embraced him, throwing up their gang set.

"I almost had one of them little niggas, son." Bloody shook his head, mad at himself for letting 50 slip his grip like that. Bloody knew he had the upper hand, but he fumbled.

"Who dat?"

"The 50 nigga, fam," Bloody shot back.

"Damn, dawg. It's cool, don't trip, we gonna get another chance."

"I be knowing, homie, but check this out. I want to open shop in Stafford again and Woodbridge, but this time, flood them hoods with our homies. Lock that shit down," Bloody said seriously.

"You sure, bruh? That's going to be a nasty showdown, dawg. You saw what happened to our crew in Stafford." Jeezy knew Bloody was tripping now.

"That's why I say flood the area with our guys, we gonna muscle our way in. It's no more nice guys, bro, we about to take over. We got the army, money, and weapons." Bloody was trying to get his boy to see shit his way.

"Ok. I'mma put that shit together, but I think Richmond and Bad News is good enough, because now we'll be stepping on more toes," Jeezy said.

"Toes are meant to be stepped on, son. That's a fact, and I don't trust you to think, homie, I trust you to do as I say." Bloody got in his truck, leaving Jeezy there.

***

Stafford, VA

Capo posted up outside of a Taco Bell fast-food restaurant, leaning on his car smoking a blunt of exotic weed he got from his white boy weed plug from the west coast.

Don and 50 set up a little meeting with Capo and Tank Brim, so they could put their little differences to the side. Everybody thought it was for the best since they were all on the team now, and didn't nobody want bad blood in the circle. Capo agreed to meet with Tank Brim, even though he disliked the man, but he did respect his gun play.

A white Cadillac with rims pulled into the small lot blasting a 21 Savage album. Tank Brim hopped out, dressed in all red with a necklace in diamonds that read Brim.

Capo loved his Crip set, but he wasn't on no shit like Tank Brim. He had to admit Tank Brim reminded him of Tech before he was murdered by Bree.

"What's up, dawg," Tank Brim addressed Capo, keeping his distance just in case he tried to black Capo.

Coming down here to meet Capo was hard, but he did it for 50, and since they were all as one now, Tank Brim wanted to play fair.

"Glad you came out, bruh, but first, let me clear the air. That shit me and you had was petty. We on a bigger level now and we all on the same team, so I'm down to put bygones in the past," Capo stated, being the bigger person.

"I feel you, dawg, and I'm down for that." Tank Brim extended his hand and Capo shook it, unaware of the black minivan that just snuck into the lot.

Tat!!
Tat!!
Tat!!

Tat!!

Tat!!

Capo was quick to react. He pushed Tank Brim out the way and dodged the bullets from the MP5 assault rifles.

Boom!

Boom!

Boom!

Capo hit one of the shooters hanging out of the van's sliding doors. There were two more shooters, but not for long, because Tank Brim hit both targets.

The van raced off with only the driver inside. Three men lay on the pavement, but one was still alive, trying his best to crawl to freedom. Capo ran down on the shooter, kicking his face.

"Who sent you on this dummy mission?" Capo asked.

"Jeezy, man, please I…"

Boom!

Boom!

Boom!

Capo looked at Tank Brim like, who the fuck is Jeezy?

"I know him, bruh. I'll fill you in later, we gotta get from around here." Tank Brim saw people calling the police from inside Taco Bell.

Both men left in their cars. Tank Brim had heard of Jeezy. He was a blood dude from Richmond with ties to Bad News. He knew Jeezy's gang was heavy in Bad News and all over VA, so he knew this could be bigger than it seemed.

Romell Tukes

Chapter 15
Dale City, VA

The whole crew was in Don's crib grilling food and drinking, having a good time for Lil' PJ's birthday. Don bought him a $170K watch and Capo bought him a Lambo truck he was loving already.

"Don, what we gonna do about this new Jeezy kid?" Capo mentioned.

"Where did he even come from?" Lil' PJ said, drinking out of a white foam cup.

"He probably the nigga who killed Rugs," 50 stated, remembering the man's face who tried to kill him.

"Y'all said he a blood, right?" Don asked, looking at Tank Brim, who was the only person there who heard of Jeezy.

"Yeah," Tank Brim confirmed, cooking on the grill and acting like he was the cook, but he loved cooking and he had skills.

"I think Bloody also a blood, and Twin, so find out if there is any connection, because everything seems a little off not to be connected," Don told everybody.

"Aight, that's too easy. Me and Tank got that." Capo took a sip on lean he'd been addicted to for some time now.

"I'm glad everybody here, because I want to make an announcement," Don stated, catching everybody's attention.

"This shit better be good." Capo looked at Don.

"I'm going to New York for a while to meet my father's side of the family, because I believe there's more to Rich than what he was telling. I'm also going to look into this Bloody nigga while I'm up there." Don had been planning this trip since he was locked up, but he'd been waiting for the right time.

When Don would spin the yard in prison with his dad, Rich, before he killed him, Rich used to tell him about his family in Brooklyn. Rich would leave out a lot of details, which used to leave Don in a loophole.

"When we leaving?" 50 asked seriously, needing a small vacation, and he always wanted to go to New York. 50 met a lot of New York cats in VA, and the stories they used to tell him made him put New York on his bucket list.

"Nah, 50, I gotta go by myself on this one," Don stated.

"You think that's smart? You outta turf, bruh, you should take someone with you." Lil' PJ knew Don was tripping for real.

"I need all of you here and I need you to handle the drug operations again until I get back," Don told Lil' PJ, who disagreed with Don's plans, but he was gonna always back up his boy.

"We got you," Capo said, because everybody else didn't know what to say.

The rest of the night, they went out to a few clubs and turned up for Lil' PJ's birthday and Don's going away party.

***

Richmond, VA

BK walked outta the soul food spot he'd just had a meeting at with CL about a connect. CL called his people in NY right in front of BK at the table while eating. CL's people in NY spoke very highly of BK and how he was one of the biggest brick layers in the city. What CL couldn't figure out or add up was how could a man like BK with his status need a plug if he was already a source.

Being in the game so long, CL knew how easy it was to fall from the top to the bottom overnight. He thought that was

BK's story, at least he hoped so, because he agreed to do business with him.

BK left a happy man with new plans to get a piece of Bad News, but his first plan he had was to build a crew, and he knew of the right people.

***

Hampton, VA

Twin dropped off his first shipment to his little soldiers in a small project area in Hampton known for its heavy drug trafficking. His plan wasn't hard. He came up with the idea to take drugs from CL and build his own empire while taking over CL's turf. He knew he had to play the background, so his hand could never be exposed, or it could backfire. Hunting down Don and the crew took up too much of his time. His focus now screamed money. Walking to his car, he heard someone.

"Whoooooops…" Twin heard the blood and shouted back.

"Whoop," he shouted back, seeing a man approach him dressed in a red Givenchy outfit.

"What's poppin', blood. I'm Bloody 9trey, the big homie from NY. I need to holler at you, son," Bloody said, having Twin's full attention.

Twin heard of Bloody, his name was heavy in their 9trey set.

"Let's talk," Twin stated as they got into a deep conversation for two hours and made plans to team up.

Romell Tukes

Chapter 16
Arlington County Jail
Three Months Later

Melly sat in the prison van staring out the window as the van pulled back into the jail. Today he had a speedy trial hearing and blew trial to get a life sentence plus forty years for killing a cop. He couldn't believe his ears when the judge offered him all that time. The only person who came to his court date was one of his exes who was following his high-profile case.

When the judge gave him his time, his ex was jumping up and down, laughing and even twerking in the back. For some reason, tears couldn't fall down his face because it was mainly his heart crying.

The van waited outside the prison, waiting its turn to go inside. He now wished he would've left the street life alone and lived a square life once Big Bio died, as he wanted to.

***

Brooklyn, NY

Don had a nice skyrise condo in the Park Slope area overlooking the Hudson River and Manhattan. Since he'd been in NY, he'd been doing his research and learning the city day by day. All he had to go off was a couple of names and locations his father used to speak of while they would walk the prison yard together.

Every day Don thought back to the day he killed his father, Rich, in the prison shower. He could never forget the look on his face. He hated rats and snakes, and Rich turned out to be two in one.

Today he had plans to meet the man who claimed to be Rich's dad and his grandfather. Asking a couple of questions

69

to the right people got him in touch with the man. Word on the streets was he was a serious OG with a lot of power and money. Don had forty minutes before his lunch meeting at a downtown restaurant.

***

Downtown Brooklyn, NY

Don got out of the Uber in a nice designer suit with a pair of Tom Ford sunglasses on. The restaurant had a nice, fancy touch to it as he walked inside, to see two big, black gorillas standing in suits. He had no clue who he was looking for, all he had was a name, Rick.

"Follow us," one of the men said, taking him to a private section of the restaurant, passing tables filled with the rich and wealthy.

When he walked into the area, he saw seven goons surrounding an older light-skinned man with gray hair and glasses, eating soup.

"Sit," the man said with his voice relaxed. Rick looked at Don for at least a full sixty seconds before telling his goons to leave.

Don sat at the end of the table, seeing the resemblance in the man's face and eyes. He knew they shared the same bloodline.

"You want something to eat?" Rick asked.

"I'm straight," Don replied.

"So, you killed my son and your own father?" Rick asked before taking a sip of water.

"Yeah, and I'd do it again."

"You got a real big heart coming out here. What if I choose not to let you make it back to VA?" Rick asked.

"Then it is what it is. I'll die with honor." Don looked Rick in his cold eyes.

"I know you're my grandson now," Rick said with a smile.

"I just want answers," Don stated.

"I'll give you everything you need, but I'm glad you killed that son of a bitch," Rick said, upset.

"How did Rich come to VA?" Don asked.

"Your family is heavy into the drug game. I have a lot of sons and daughters all over the world. Our roots run deep into the motherland," Rick repeated.

"Damn."

"Don't think because your mom was white you was," Rick laughed.

"The blacker the better."

"True, but your father was a piece of shit. I showed him the game at an early age, so he was very advanced. I used to send him to VA with his brother and family. One year he got caught with some sit and ratted and brought down a whole block of mine, and two of your cousins still doing a life bid in the feds." Rick saw Don's shocked look. Had he known that, he would have been killed him.

"Then, he stole a lot of keys from me and went to VA and built himself an empire. Family, no offense on you, but that's why I never reached out to you," Rick said.

"No tears lost," Don replied.

"Your father has another son. He's a piece of shit also, but he's not a rat, he's a troublemaker." Rick hated Bloody for trying to fuck his wife.

"Tell me about him," Don said as Rick went into detail about Bloody's whole life.

Romell Tukes

Chapter 17
Woodbridge, VA

"Dis nigga only been outchea a couple of months and got bricks snowing all over the place," 50 said, watching an apartment complex ran by Bloody and Jeezy.

50 and the crew had been laying low, doing their homework on Bloody and Jeezy and now Twin, because they saw him hanging out with the duo.

"Bruh a hustler. I give him that. He just stepped on the wrong toes," Lil' PJ said, paying close attention to all the trafficking going on in the section 8, low-income housing area.

"I can't believe he's Don's brother." 50 was glad they had different fathers now.

"Me neither, but yo, you ready?" Lil' PJ lifted his AR-15 assault rifle, which recently became his weapon of choice.

"Why you always using that big goofy?" 50 grabbed his Glock 23 with a 30-round clip at the bottom.

"Same reason everybody wanna to use a Draco and chopper, dawg." Lil' PJ didn't like when people questioned his ways.

"Aight, I'm ready. How you want to do this?" 50 asked.

"We gonna air this bitch, bruh, what the fuck you mean?" Lil' PJ saw eight hustlers standing outside trapping.

Yayo posted up on the block as he did every day of the year. He was recently selling nicks and dime bags of weed, now he had bricks moving left and right. Jeezy and Yayo grew up together when they stayed in Richmond. Yayo had his hood on lock. He already opened three traps all around Woodbridge.

"I'll be right back," Yayo told his guys, leaving to go across town to see what his mom wanted because she recently texted him. When he got inside his car, he heard gunfire.

Tat!
Tat!
Tat!
Tat!
Boc!
Boc!
Tat!
Tat!
Tat!
Boc!
Boc!
Boc!

Yayo saw two shooters and pulled off while bullets hit the trunk of his car. He sold drugs, he wasn't a killer or gangsta. He called Jeezy on speaker phone, speeding away from his hood in fear, shaking while trying to control the steering wheel.

***

Richmond, VA

Brooke, or as her coworkers knew her, Agent Brooke, realized her car needed an oil change. She drove to the nearest oil place in her neighborhood, which was located a few blocks away from her home.

Her cocoa butter skin, brown eyes, silky hair, and cute face made every male try their hand, but she wasn't going for it. Being alone and single was perfect for her so she could focus on her rising career with the FBI in Richmond. At twenty-nine, her life and goals were in order. She fit the title as a boss bitch.

Seeing the new tire and oil change shop on the next corner, she made a right, seeing it was still open. Getting off work overnight at 6 pm gave her time to wine and dine by herself. Work took a toll on her, but she loved it, not because she could arrest bad guys, but so she could bring justice to the streets. Being from the rough streets of Richmond, she knew the streets better than most of her coworkers.

Her brother, Jeezy, was a known drug dealer and gang member throughout Richmond. She had little respect for him because he always had a bright future, but he chose the streets.

"Excuse me, are you still open?" she asked the man who looked as if he planned to close the shop.

"Come on, ma, I got you." The man made her smile because nobody ever called her ma.

"Thank you."

"Pull your car into the garage. What you need, an oil change?" he asked.

"Yes."

"Aight." The man went to get everything ready to drain her old oil and replace it with new oil.

"Nice car." The man looked at her new BMW.

"It's not better than your Benz," she replied, staring at the man who she found very attractive, which was rare.

"I guess you right." He made her laugh.

"What's your name? I can tell you not from around here." She could tell by his accent.

"My name is Kirk, I'm from NY."

"A Yankee, ok, this must be your shop," she asked, looking around.

"Yeah, I own a couple. Just trying to make it," BK said.

"I bet." They talked until he got done, and they ended up exchanging numbers, feeling each other's energy and vibes.

Chapter 18
Richmond, VA

Tank Brim walked around the mall to do a little shopping. Something he hadn't been able to do since he'd been so busy. Teaming up with Lil' PJ and Capo made shit a little easier for him and 50, because he felt as if they were alone. He had strong ties to every blood set in VA, so he did more research on Jeezy and this Bloody cat.

That's why he came out to Richmond to meet up with his homie, Five, who told him he had some information for him. 50 wanted to come, but Tank Brim told him to chill with Jazzy, he could handle himself. With Lil' PJ supplying the work now, he and 50 still had traps booming while in a time of war. He spent another $20,000 at the mall, shopping mainly for sneakers and hats. He also got a couple of women's phone numbers.

Once outside, the heat burned his skin. It was so hot today. He looked at his Rolex watch, realizing Five was supposed to have been here twenty minutes ago. He figured Five got a little scared and backed out. He was always a scary nigga.

Out of nowhere, a gang of men jumped out of a Tahoe SUV with big guns, and Tank Brim quickly pulled out his weapon.

Boc!

Boc!

Boc!

Boc!

Tank Brim shot two of the men in the face, but the other three gunmen let up with no mercy.

Tat!

Tat!

Tat!
Tat!
Tat!

Tank Brim hid behind cars, running from the bullets his handgun couldn't match up to. A Kia sedan pulled up to him and pushed the door open so he could get inside.

"Damn, Five, where *you* come from?" Tank Brim asked, glad Five saved him.

"I just got here, bruh. You straight?" Five asked, driving out the mall lot.

"Hell nah, niggas just tried to take me out," he shot back, looking out the back window to see if they were being followed.

"I know." Five pulled over on the side of the road. Tank Brim looked at him as if he lost his mind.

Five pulled out a gun and pointed it at Tank Brim.

"I'm sorry, but you barked up da wrong tree, homie. Jeezy my big fool, and you put me in a bad situation," Five said as his phone rang to see it was Jeezy calling.

When Five got the call from Tank Brim asking about Jeezy, his big homie, he called Jeezy minutes later. Jeezy told him to tell Tank Brim to meet him at the local mall.

Tank Brim said nothing. He understood this was part of the game, but he was mad a sucker nigga was about to end his life.

Five pulled the trigger, but the gun jammed. When Tank Brim saw this, he punched Five in his face, then took his gun, shooting him in his face. He pushed Five's body out the car onto the road before driving off and seeing Jeezy's name pop up on the phone as he answered.

"You handle that nigga?" Jeezy asked over the phone, thinking Five picked up.

"Nah, dawg, I handled that nigga. I'll be seeing you soon, bitch ass nigga, bet that," Tank Brim said before hanging up the phone.

Jeezy drove past Five's body on the road, shaking his head. He thought he had Tank Brim set off, that's why he told Five to play the background just in case he escaped.

He had to go meet Bloody to talk about a new spot he planned to open in Dale City. He didn't plan to tell Bloody about this slip-up because it would make him look bad in front of the big homie. He didn't think it was a good idea to bring Twin into the fold because he knew how Twin got down. He moved with snakes.

When Jeezy told Bloody, he laughed and explained to Jeezy that a snake was what they needed at the moment. He left it at that and never spoke on it again.

Romell Tukes

Chapter 19
Brooklyn Heights, NY

Don waited outside the nice brownstone home in a middle-class area of Brooklyn. There wasn't a doubt in his mind that Brooklyn had it for one of the most dangerous hoods he'd ever been in.

Rick had given him everything he needed to know about Bloody, from his ex-girlfriends, baby mother, mom's info, friends, and he went so far as giving him his social security number.

Don could easily tell Rick had something against Bloody, but that wasn't his business. He got what he needed from him concerning Bloody.

Hearing Rick tell Don everything left him with an awkward feeling. His family was full of kingpins and the news overwhelmed him. Rick told him since he didn't have a real plug, he would provide him with the best on the east coast. They agreed to send the first load to VA tonight to Lil' PJ.

Don saw an older brown-skinned woman walk up the stairs into the apartment with bags in her hand. Before she made it inside, he got out of the car to help the woman.

"Let me help you," he said, helping her with the bags.

"Thank you, young man." When the woman saw Don's face, she paused because he looked just like Rich, her first lover and everything.

"No problem." Don pulled out his weapon and fired six shots into Bloody's mom's face, leaving her body to collapse on the porch.

***

Richmond, VA

Bloody sat down in some raggedy apartment while some chicken head with a crazy head game sucked his pole for an hour straight. The woman had her period, so sex wasn't happening. Running red lights made her feel nastier than she already was.

His phone rang while he was moaning, and he didn't want to pick up, but he stopped the woman and answered the phone.

"Yo, talk nice," he answered his cousin's call. Seconds later, he had tears in his eyes as his phone dropped to the floor after hearing his mom got killed.

***

Greenville Prison, VA

Melly arrived at the prison on a Friday, and the population was locked down for the weekend. He heard a lot about the prison, and it wasn't good, but he knew this was what he had to get used to for the rest of his life.

He tried not to think about his life sentence in prison, but he couldn't help not to think about it. Being locked in the cell all day drove him crazy, but today he was coming out for an hour with the rest of the unit.

Melly's door popped open and he rushed to the prison phone, which was posted on a wall next to his cell. He called his ex-girl who had his money at her house. Before he got arrested, she was his ride or die and he took good care of her. When she picked up the phone, Melly's face glowed with happiness.

"What's up, baby," he told her.

"Melly, why are you calling me so early," she shot back in her wake-up voice.

"My bad, babe. I miss you."

"Melly, I can't do this shit."

"Huh." He thought he was hearing shit.

"I can't do this time with you."

"What? You told me you always had my back," he stated, fearing this day would come as niggas told him.

"I said that at the moment, Melly. I got kids, and I found someone who loves me," she said, crushing his heart.

"Look, just send me my fucking money, bitch." When he said those words, the phone went dead...

When he turned around, Pookie rushed him with a big knife, stabbing him in his stomach, face, and heart for over sixty seconds. By the time the corrections officers ran into the unit, Melly laid on the floor, bleeding to death. Pookie swung his knife at the guards, stabbing two of them in the neck. They eventually placed Pookie in cuffs, taking him away as nurses flooded the unit trying to save the COs, but one of them died next to Melly.

Romell Tukes

Chapter 20
Richmond, VA

Mrs. Ford left the Walmart shopping center pushing a cart full of organic food. She wanted to try something new other than fried food or soul food. Not only that, but her doctor told her she had high blood pressure, which was shocking news to her because she took her health seriously. She stayed in the gym daily and was a yoga instructor at a local fitness center her husband owned.

Brooke and Jeezy were her children, who she loved to death. Even though her son lived a life she highly disapproved of, she still loved him. She also had another son in high school who was the best quarterback in the state. He had a bright future.

After loading up her car with the bags, she made her way home to cook for Mr. Ford, her husband, whom she loved with all her heart. Tonight was their 30th anniversary, and she planned to let him fuck her brains out all over the house. She was 50 years old, but her body was tight and toned.

"Damn, bruh, for an old bitch, shawty nice. I can't lie, dawg, what you think?" Lil' P said as they followed Mrs. Ford's luxury car.

"She nice. I wonder if she got any daughters?" Capo puzzled.

"I'll fuck the shit outta them if she did, believe dat." Lil' PJ tried to keep up with the woman, who was speeding through traffic like a mad woman.

Capo and Lil' PJ had been keeping tabs on Jeezy's mom for some days, and today they planned to handle their business.

Don had tons of bricks he'd been sending to Lil' PJ, and the grade of the heroin they were getting had the fiends itching for more.

"How Don get a plug that fast? He only been in NY for a couple of months, bruh," Capo asked Lil' PJ, as if he knew.

"Shit, hell if I know, but whatever he did, I'm glad, because we all about to be way up," Lil' PJ stated, seeing Mrs. Ford pull into a driveway of a nice middle-class suburban home.

"Let's make this quick." Capo saw her about to get out the car, and they rushed her with weapons.

When Mrs. Ford saw the two men coming, she screamed, trying to run, but the bullets knocked her down.

Boc!
Boc!
Boc!

Lil' PJ stood over her, dumping shots into her head. They ran off leaving the scene, forgetting what just took place.

"When we going out to Miami?" Capo asked.

"Right now," Lil' PJ confirmed.

"Now?"

"Yeah, I already told 50 to take care of the drug operations, so we good. Drive to the airport." Lil' PJ couldn't wait to get out of VA for a while.

"Aight." Capo drove to the airport with no more questions asked.

***

FBI Building, Richmond
Two Weeks Later

Today was Brooke's first day back to work since the death of her mother. Burying her mom was the hardest thing she had to do in her whole life. When she saw all the gunshot wounds to her mother's back and head, she knew the murder was personal.

"Agent Brooke, I'm sorry to hear about the loss of your mother. If you need a few more weeks or days off, you're excused with pay. You're our best," her boss stated.

"Thank you, boss, but I'm ok, and I appreciate the flowers and kind gestures," Brooke told him.

Her boss was an African American man in his early 30s, very smart and handsome with no kids and no wife. She knew he always liked her, but he wasn't her type. For some reason, she had a thing for bad boys, but she couldn't get Kirk out of her mind.

"Let me know if you need anything, don't be scared to ask." Her boss walked off, leaving her to her work. He just wanted to comfort her the best he could and win brownie points.

Brooke shook her head because she knew what he was trying to do. Feed off her hurt and pain. She tossed his flowers in the dumpster. She planned to look into the files of the most dangerous murderers and kingpins in the city to see if she could find any motive or connect dots. The first person she planned to start with was CL… A man who had been on the FBI shit list for years.

Romell Tukes

Chapter 21
Virginia Beach, VA

Capo came back from Miami two nights ago, and he had a blast down there for a whole week. He loved everything about Miami, and he couldn't wait to go back to South Beach. He even did the basketball tournament out there and killed it. He posted up in the back of the club, drinking with four Crips from his hood. It was Christmas weekend, so the city of Virginia Beach was off the hook.

People from all over came out to have a good time partying. Capo had his eyes on one person that was his main purpose of being out in the club tonight, besides fucking with some bad bitch he came across. He focused on the man buying all the bottles from the bar, turning up with his crew. He didn't have plans to get him tonight, he just wanted to keep tabs on the man who was CL's cousin and right-hand man.

Looking toward the bar, Capo saw a sexy brown-skinned bitch with a fat ass and a very familiar face, but he couldn't match her face.

Lucky had a crew of shooters at the bar with him by his side and a couple of women he just met. One woman stood out to him. She had a crazy body, but her face stood out. Lucky had a lot of bad bitches in his life, but this one had to be killing all of them.

Lucky had a cocky attitude with a pretty boy swag. Born and raised in Virginia Beach, he considered himself the king of the city. His cousin and best friend, CL, was dropping 200 to 300 keys in his lap every other week.

"What's up, shawdy, you trying to get up outta here, just me and you?" he asked the woman whose name he didn't know yet.

"How about I'm Treasure," the woman said with an attitude.

"I'm Pleasure, nice to meet you," he shot back, making her break a smile.

"Oh, Pleasure, huh, is that a myth or the truth?" She played his game.

"How about we go find out?"

"I'm always down for an interesting challenge." She got up and left the club with him.

Lucky drove back to his condo in his Ferrari, feeling on her thick thighs. When he felt a fat, shaved pussy, his manhood grew hard, especially to the sounds of her moans.

She cocked her legs wide open as he drove, playing in her tightness. He couldn't even fit two fingers inside of the tight womb.

"Mmmm." She reached in his lap, pulling out his dick, and started kissing and sucking on the tip, making him pull over on the highway.

"Oh my god," he cried out as she went back and forth on his dick, making him bust in her mouth with her slow sucking tactics.

When he came, she spit his kids back on his dick and reached under his seat where she saw him put his weapon earlier. Lucky was so amazed, he couldn't wait to get Treasure back to his crib. Treasure came up from his lap.

Boc!
Boc!
Boc!
Boc!
Boc!

The bullets rested in his chest, killing him. She pushed him out of the car before taking off. Treasure was really Lil' Two. She thought she'd just killed CL, but that was his cousin. She couldn't wait to tell Tank Brim, because he didn't have faith in her, but she planned to do everything to prove him wrong.

Even if she had to suck and fuck, which she hated, but she wanted to prove her loyalty. She saw Capo in the club. She'd seen him many times and always had a crush on him. He was the only male she ever desired.

***

Brooklyn, NY

Irina and her daughter, who at twelve years old stood close to six feet tall like her mother, were out shopping. Irina had to pick up some last-minute things from Macy's shopping center for Christmas. Today, the snow in the city was not as bad as the previous days where she couldn't even get out the driveway to do her last-minute shopping. Like most NYers, last-minute shopping was a tradition.

Irina's brother was Bloody and the two had an odd relationship, but they still loved each other dearly.

"Time to go. Your eyes are starting to wander too much. I spent seven hundred dollars on your black ass," Irina told her daughter, who she spoiled because she made good grades in school.

Outside, they saw a man standing near the store in a Santa Claus suit begging for money with a bell.

"Mommy?"

"What?" Irina said, counting the money she got back from the store clerk because she was short seven dollars.

"Mommy, can we give poor Santa some money?" her daughter asked.

"Hell nah, we ain't put that nigga there, and a lot of them poor Santas be scamming here, girl. This Brooklyn, not Hollywood." Irina shook her head at the man in disgust.

"Please, Mommy?"

"Ok. Come on." Irina gave in, pulling out two dollars for the man.

When the man saw this, he looked at Irina and so did her daughter, who couldn't believe her mom's selfish ways on the holiday season.

"Merry Christmas, hoe," Santa said.

"Excuse me, nigga." Irina heard what he said, she just wanted to make sure.

Santa pulled out a gun and shot Irina and her daughter before running off. Don had been waiting in the cold for an hour for Irina.

Chapter 22
Bad News, VA

Sean was BK's cousin, and he'd been in Bad News hustling for years, mostly selling weed and molly. Since BK came to VA, shit had been going his way now. He was moving ounces and grams of dope outta his little brother Millz's house on the northside. Once BK told him that CL was supplying him, he knew they were about to be on, but the only issue was the competition.

Sean knew about CL's beef with Don's crew, the whole city did, and he didn't want any parts of that. He never met CL or Don personally, but the stories he heard through the mean streets let him know they weren't to be fucked with.

"Yo, I'm about to bounce, cuz, you straight?" Sean asked his cousin and little brother sitting in the living room, counting money they made today.

"I got two bricks left. When you going to come through for me?" his little brother Vado asked.

"I'm seeing BK tomorrow, stay down until then." Sean then left the crib.

"Who the fuck is this nigga, bruh? Why niggas keep popping up out here, man? It's some funny shit going on, and I ain't feeling this shit," Capo told 50, watching Sean come out the apartment.

"Where the fuck is this Chinese food at, fool? I'm starving," Vado said, flicking through the TV for a movie to watch until his clients called for some work.

He heard the doorbell ring and sent his little homie to answer the door.

"If that shit cold again, don't tip that cat-eating motherfucker," Vado yelled.

When the door opened, the man thought he saw a ghost until his brains got splattered all over the hallway walls. Vado heard the gunfire and grabbed his gun under his couch.

Boc!

Boc!

Boc!

50 side stepped the bullets and ducked while Vado let off two more shots at 50, but Vado was unaware of Capo's presence.

Boom!

The shotgun blast hit Vado in his side, dropping him to the floor as both men ran down on him, kicking his gun across the floor.

"Please," Vado cried, spitting out blood.

"Who runs this operation?" Capo asked, pointing the shotgun to Vado's face.

"Sean and BK," Vado managed to get out before he coughed on his own blood, dying.

"Who is BK?" 50 asked.

"We will find out." Capo left, picking up a blunt of weed on the living room table.

BK had a busy day at his bike store in Bad News. He sold over twenty motorcycles in December. He knew putting all bikes on sale at half price would bring people out, and it did.

He and Brooke had been on three dates already, and he was really feeling her because she had class and sex appeal. He loved everything about her. She told him she worked for the state, so he knew she had a good job and didn't want him for his money. The bricks CL had been tossing him, he was pushing them off to Sean and his cousin in Richmond.

Sean text him earlier, letting him know he had to speak to him. BK didn't like speaking on the phone because he saw a lot of good men get caught up on wiretaps talking crazy. Sean walked in the store and BK brought him to the back and told his two employees to hold down the front.

"We ran into a problem last night. Niggas killed my little brother and cuz last night." Sean's voice was saddened.

"Shit, do you know who?"

"A fiend told me he saw Capo leaving the apartment around that time." Sean shook his head.

"Who dat?"

"He wit' Don's crew, bruh. It's all bad, they on to us. I knew it, this was the shit I feared. This is why I never sold dog food, bruh. Them niggas don't play about this shit."

"Chill out, son, I'mma figure something out, just lay low. I gotta get back to work. I'll hit you in a few days," BK told him, escorting him out the store.

Romell Tukes

Chapter 23
Hampton, VA

"Uhmmm, damn, ma," Bloody moaned with his hands behind his head, watching Jaden suck him off, going ham on the dick.

Jaden spit on the tip and went deep until his rod touched her throat. She tongued the base with his whole pipe in her mouth. He met Jaden at a club two nights ago. She saw he had on all red and approached him, letting him know she was blood also. They met at a hole-in-the-wall hotel in the hood twenty minutes ago, and she'd been sucking dick since.

She filled the room with slurping sounds until he shot a load in her mouth, watching her catch all his kids.

"I'm using da bathroom real quick, and then I'ma come ride that pipe. I'm on birth control, so you can cum inside me," she said, getting up naked as her big breasts bounced.

"I was gonna do dat anyway, ma," Bloody said, watching her go into the bathroom with her phone. He hurried up and got dressed in a rush before he heard the toilet flush. He stood on the side of the bathroom door with his gun out, listening to her text. He kicked the door open with his Timbs to catch her texting.

Boc!

Boc!

Boc!

Boc!

The bullets landed in Jaden's head, instantly killing her. Bloody took her phone and saw Tank Brim's name and a text saying, "Hurry up, baby, I just gave him head. He laying down, come on, hurry."

Bloody texted, "nice try blood," and ran out the hotel room, leaving the scene. Bloody saw Jaden leave the club the night he met her, climbing in a car with Tank Brim, so he was hip to her.

Tank Brim stopped at a red light, seeing a red BMW speed past his Toyota. He read the text from Jaden and when he saw the last part, he cursed himself. He then thought about the red BMW that just sped past him. Tank Brim didn't even go to the hotel because he knew his ex, Jaden, was dead.

***

Brooklyn, NY

Don arrived in a nice middle-class neighborhood called Cobble Hill, which was filled with nice brownstones. He had on his Santa suit with two boxes wrapped up nice gift wrap.

Today NY had close to six inches of snow outside. He hated the cold weather, but he had no choice at the moment. Later, Rick wanted to meet up with him again downtown near his hotel.

Lil' PJ had been sending Rick the money through Cashapp, so business on his end was good. Right now, Don had to take care of something more important. He climbed out the hooptie in his Santa suit and boots, making his way to the stairs. He rang the doorbell twice with two boxes of gifts in his hand.

A beautiful Puerto Rican came to the door with a young boy. Her beauty and curves stood out to Don, and he had to control his lust.

"Hohoho, merry Christmas," Don shouted in his best Santa voice.

"Thank you," she said.

"These are for y'all." Don passed her the gifts.

"This is so sweet," she said before he fired two rounds in her head and her son's face.

Don got back in his hooptie, driving through the snow trying to prevent his car from spinning. It was so bad outside.

***

Bad News, VA

Capo was waiting in the bowling alley for Tank Brim to show up so they could go bowling. Tank Brim walked in the spot with another nigga, but when they got closer, Capo remembered the face, and it was not a nigga.

"What's up, dawg." Tank Brim embraced Capo.

"What's poppin', cuz," Capo said, looking at the tomboy whose beauty was beyond alluring.

"This my cuz, she gonna be working with us. She solid." Tank Brim pointed at Lil' Two, who made quick eye contact, feeling her panties soak up at the man she desired.

"Let's bowl," Capo said, feeling a vibe with Lil' Two, but keeping it to himself. They bowled and went out to eat, making plans for their next mission on Bloody and this new BK nigga.

Romell Tukes

Chapter 24
Richmond, VA

Kay left the hospital where she worked as an assistant nurse, to go pick up her son from her mom's house across town. Her beauty spoke for itself. She was a sexy brown-skinned woman focused on a bag and her career.

She was CL's baby mother to their one-year-old son. CL hadn't done anything for her and his son since she had him. He'd only seen him one time, which pissed her off, but she planned to raise her child by herself. She never needed a nigga, she believed in being strong minded and independent.

After picking up her son, she was going to take him to her sister's crib so she could hit the gym and get rid of her body fat. All her friends and sister told her to get a tummy tuck, but she refused because she knew the gym would get her back fine again. She stopped at a nearby gas station because she just realized her tank read empty.

Lil' PJ and Tank Brim rode a couple of cars behind Kay, pulling into the gas station.

"Do you think letting Capo and Lil' Two work together gonna be ok?" Tank Brim asked, because they both were loose cannons.

"I hope so, but Capo ain't as dumb as he looks. They got a little funny vibe when they around each other. I never saw Capo act so weird."

"I never seen Lil' Two act that way. I don't know, but fuck all that, bruh. How you want to do this?" Tank Brim asked, seeing Kay walk into the gas station to get gas.

"Let's wait until she pull out and get her at the entrance." Lil' PJ saw the cameras all over the store, so he didn't want to be on tape.

Kay pumped her gas and got back in her car. When she made it to the exit way, a car pulled up on the side of her.

Boc!

Boc!

Boc!

Boc!

Boc!

Boc!

The bullets tore through her driver door, hitting her six times in her organs, killing her.

***

Bad News, VA

Today Capo and Lil' Two both were focused on their first mission together. They both wore black outfits for their night time drill.

"This nigga open up a new trap every day out here," Capo said to himself, but hoping Lil' Two replied as she played in her phone.

He couldn't help but feel Lil' Two. She had everything he wanted in a woman, and he never forgot about the day he saw her body in that dress in the club.

Lil' Two didn't say a word, she just watched the trap house, seeing the same two fiends run in and out for the last two hours.

"That night I saw you at the club, what happened to CL's cousin?"

"What you think?" Lil' Two shot back with an attitude because she was on her period.

"Aight." Capo made a note to himself not to ask her shit else.

"Why do you look at me like that?" she asked.

"Huh?"

"You heard me." Lil' Two knew she caught him off guard.

"I-I-I-I don't know what you talking about, but I think we should make our move." Capo fumbled over his words, seeing her smirk as she picked up her Tech 9 submachine gun.

They got out of the SUV about to cross the street, but Capo heard a noise in the bushes, making him turn around to see Bloody and two gunmen.

"Two..." Capo shouted, blocking Lil' Two and catching a bullet to his shoulder. She was quick on her draw.

Tat!

Tat!

Tat!

Tat!

She took out one of the gunmen and went for Bloody. Capo shot at the other shooter running and tripping off the curb.

Boc!

Boc!

Capo put two rounds in the gunman's back, then dodged Bloody's rainfall of bullets.

Tat!

Tat!

Tat!

Lil' Two saw Bloody run back into the woods. Little did they know, he had his eyes on them the whole time. They left the scene and she took Capo to the hospital in Hampton and stayed there with him all night because he saved her life.

Romell Tukes

Chapter 25

Bad News, VA

Bloody smoked on an ounce of loud thinking about what happened to his baby mother and seed recently. He knew someone in VA had to have connections with someone in NY, because it wasn't adding up that now his loved ones were dying out of nowhere.

When his sister died, he thought it could have been anybody, maybe mistaken identity, but once he heard about his baby mother and child, he knew it had to be a hit. In NY, he had no enemies he knew of because they were all dead, so he knew it had to be his recent actions in VA biting him in his ass now.

"What's up, dawg, you ready to slide to DC?" Jeezy walked into the apartment and saw him blowing loud.

Jeezy could feel his boy's pain after losing his sister, baby mother, and seed. When he recently lost his mom, he felt his world flipped upside down. He knew Don's crew had to be the cause of all of this, and Bloody argued and vowed to kill everything they loved.

"I'm getting dressed." Bloody went to get dressed in the back so he could go to DC to pick up money from his workers.

Jeezy took a seat on the couch where Bloody was just sitting and saw lines of coke on a mirror. He didn't know Bloody was getting high, but he could tell there was a change in his mood. Jeezy got back up, paying the drugs no mind because he knew nobody was perfect.

***

Richmond, VA

Agent Brooke had been working late trying to find out who was responsible for her mom's death. She had a feeling the death could have been because of Jeezy's street life, but she planned to save her wild card until the time was right. She checked her watch to see it was past 11:30 pm, so she shut off her computer and got her belongings together to leave her office.

Brooke's main focus had been on CL. She had a couple of coworkers looking into him with her. Her goal was to open a new case on CL and build something so strong that he would never see daylight outside of a federal prison wall. If he wasn't the cause of her mom's death, then she knew he knew who was, and she wasn't stopping until she found out.

Leaving the floor, she took the elevator to the lobby.

"Have a good night, Agent Brooke," one of the security guards said, standing at his post.

"Same to you guys," she shot back in her sweet voice, carrying her work bag outside.

There were a couple of cars in the parking lot at this hour, unlike in the daytime where a person couldn't even find parking. Kirk had been texting her all day, but she hadn't had time to reply back. She had a strong feeling about him. He made her feel loved and special again, and she needed that.

Before getting to her car, a van door slid open.

Boc!

Boc!

Boc!

Brooke dropped her bag and pulled out her work weapon, shooting back on one knee like she was trained.

Boc!

Boc!

She hit one of the shooters in the waist, but she and the other shooter went back and forth. The two security guards came out shooting to help Brooke. The shooters got back in the van, racing out the lot hitting 95 mph. Her heart raced non-stop.

"You ok?"

"Yeah, call it in," she told the guards.

"Fuck, this shit, burn!" Tank Brim shouted, taking off the vest.

"How the fuck y'all miss?" Capo said, driving down the expressway trying not to laugh at Tank Brim, who cried in pain.

Capo had a cast on his left arm and Tank Brim had been laughing at him for days, now it backfired.

"I don't know. I almost had her pretty ass," 50 repeated.

"Yo, Tank, you need some muscle rub, cuz?" Capo laughed.

"Haha, nigga, just drive." Tank Brim thought the vest would prevent any pain from a bullet, but he felt like he got shot.

Romell Tukes

Chapter 26
Brooklyn, NY

Don spoke to Rick, and he informed him that one of his uncles wanted to see him, so he gave him the number. Rick told him he wasn't on good terms with his son, but he wasn't going to let that stop them from meeting.

Don arrived at a small pool hall with a bar and saw the spot had only a few people inside.

"Pardon me, but is there a Fats here?" Don asked.

"Yes, he's in the back, love," a dark-skinned bartender stated.

On his way to the back, he saw a husky man on the phone talking loud with two goons present, looking over him.

"Nephew, what's popping? Good to meet you. Y'all niggas can take a walk." Fats looked at his men.

When his goons left, Fats looked at his nephew long and hard.

"You look just like him, son. How did it feel to kill that rat nigga?" Fats asked, lighting a cigar.

"It felt good."

"When we were kids, that clown, Rich, used to snitch on me all day to our dad, so I had a feeling he was growing up to be one," Fats repeated.

"Yeah, no doubt, bruh." Don felt his vibes were a little off, but he didn't give it too much thought.

"I hear you and my nephew got some serious issues with Bloody."

"How you hear that?"

"I hear everything, pimpin'," Fats said.

"We good," Don lied.

"First, you killed y'all dad, now you trying to kill your brother. I need a nigga like you on my team," Fats stated seriously.

"I got my own team."

"I bet, but Bloody's sister, baby mother, who got the best pussy I ever had, and his seed recently got killed. I did a little investigation and you came up to NY for a reason, I might assume." Fats looked at him awkwardly.

"I don't believe that concerns you, Uncle."

"Anything that goes on in NY concerns me!" Fats shouted, getting upset by Don's smart remarks.

"I'm ending this friendly visit. I'm sure I'll see you around." Don got up and walked out the pool hall as the bartender winked and smiled at him.

***

Bad News, VA

Lil' PJ's head was spinning. He had just left one of his old chick's crib he recently started back fucking with. He spent the whole night drinking with her, but she didn't give up no pussy, which made him upset because that was his reason for coming over.

Walking to his car, he started to feel lightheaded and dizzy. He looked back to see the woman on the phone, staring at him out her living room window. His legs got weak and he didn't see the two shooters appear from the darkness.

Boc!

Boc!

Boc!

Boc!

Lil' PJ caught a shot to the leg, almost taking him down. A blue Mustang pulled up and opened fire, hitting both shooters and pulling up next to Lil' PJ.

"Get in, dummy!" 50 shouted, seeing Lil' PJ was fucked up and shot.

"50," Lil' PJ said with a slur in his voice.

"You whacked out your fucking mind. What you on, bro?" 50 asked as he thought about where he should take him so he could get his leg treated.

"I'm in pain, bruh."

"You'll be ok." 50 had been talking to Lil' PJ all day because he saw a car following him since he left the traps.

Jeezy waited for over an hour for his men to come back. He had the drop on Lil' PJ from a chick he just started fucking with. She wanted to set Lil' PJ up for some strange reason, and that's all he needed to hear. Seeing his goons weren't coming back, he pulled up to go meet Twin, who claimed he had a plan.

Romell Tukes

Chapter 27
Stafford, VA

Capo washed his body off with the shower water, which was scorching hot as he liked it. He had the drop on Twin's baby mother, who lived in Norfolk, so he and Lil' Two planned to pay her a visit.

Shit had been turned up lately. He'd been wearing a Teflon vest for safety because he didn't plan on getting shot again.

Working with Lil' Two was cool. He loved how she got down, and lately she'd been dressing like a girl, which fucked up his head, and even Tank Brim. He couldn't lie, she had the body of one of them Instagram bitches with fake asses and breasts.

He got out of the shower and went inside the bathroom to get dressed, because Lil' Two was waiting for him in his living room. When he walked into the master bedroom, he paused, shocked. Lil' Two laid on his bed naked with her legs cocked wide open, fingering her pussy, moaning his name.

"Oh my god, Capo," she moaned as he got closer, looking at the prettiest pussy he ever saw in his life.

Both of them dreamed of this day since they first laid eyes on each other. She saw Capo's sexy, chiseled frame with a towel on his waist.

"Come here," she said seductively as he made his way to her.

She took off his towel to see his penis alive. She placed her thick lips on the tip and twisted her head in circles, sucking in a slow then a fast motion.

"Shhhhhit," he moaned, standing up holding his hips.

"You like when I suck your dick?" she said, licking his pole then his balls.

"Yeah."

113

"Tell me it's mine."

"It's yours," he said the key words, then she deep-throated him. Within one minute, he came hard and she caught everything, swallowing all of it.

Capo returned the favor and ate her sweet pussy until she soaked his face with her juices. He climbed between her legs and took his time entering her love box.

"Uhmmm." She put a pillow over her screams while he got deeper in her walls.

Lil' Two's pussy muscles gripped his manhood with strength, and he felt her body tense up.

"I'm cumming, baby, oh my god," she screamed as if she was birthing a child.

Her pussy squirted all over the place before he could get his nut, but watching her squirt turned him on.

"Damn, nigga, what you stopping for? Cum in me," she said, bending over on his drenched sheets.

The sight of her fat ass made him want to marry her. He slid into her from behind, and she started dancing on his dick while her ass cheeks clapped like a stripper's. Capo came in five seconds.

***

Norfolk, VA

"She work in there?" Lil' Two asked Capo, looking at the small bar across the street.

"Yeah, she a bartender," he replied, seeing something was wrong with Lil' Two. She had the best pussy and head he ever had in his life.

"Ok," she said flatly.

"What's wrong? Since we left my spot you been acting different," he said.

"I'm not a thot. I never felt this way about a person. I'm in love with you, daddy, and I just don't want to be heartbroken," she said, wiping her tears.

"I love you too, and you wifey now." He kissed her thick lips, and she grabbed his neck, getting passionate as Twin's baby mother came out the bar.

"I got her." Lil' Two hopped out with a gun in her hand. Capo watched from the car window. He saw Lil' Two put two bullets in the middle of the pretty woman's chest, killing her.

"Who's next?" Lil' Two got back in the car.

"How about we go back to my place for round two," he said, pulling away from the murder scene.

"You read my mind, babe," she added, ready to marry him.

***

Sux 1 Prison, VA

Pookie had recently been shipped to another prison for killing Melly and a guard. He now had to do seven years in the special housing unit, which was against the law, but the prisons always did what they wanted.

Yesterday, the chaplain came by and a Muslim Imam came to turn Pookie Muslim as he requested. Pookie always wanted to become Muslim, but he lived a dangerous lifestyle and he wanted to be100% in his heart first. Now he felt as if it had to be his calling to submit to Allah. His guys, Lil' PJ and Capo, wrote him daily. He heard Don had to go up to NY for a while. Pookie still refused to take HIV meds. He didn't care because he was ready to die.

Romell Tukes

Chapter 28
Richmond, VA

Stanley tossed the football down the field to the high school running back. Stanley was the school star quarterback and Agent Brooke's little brother. Tomorrow, the school had a football game and his coach needed Stanley to focus.

He stood six feet and was lean. He had a body built for football. After football practice, he walked to his Hellcat his mother recently got for him before she got killed. Since his mom's death, he'd been living with his girlfriend, who lived near her college dorm.

"Yo, you da nice quarterback for school?" A man approached Stanley from a new Impala.

"Yeah, that's me. I ain't doing no autographs right now, bruh," Stanley said. The man laughed and Stanley felt something odd, but he continued to walk to his car.

"Yo."

"What, man?" Stanley turned around and saw the man pull out a gun.

Boc!

Boc!

Boc!

Boc!

Boc!

Lil' PJ got back inside his car, leaving Stanley's body slumped on the side of his own car. Driving back to Bad News, Lil' PJ thought about the Agent Brooke bitch and how he was gonna get her out the way before she became a problem. He knew killing a federal agent was a life sentence if he got caught, and he already slipped up once.

Jeezy was nowhere to be found in the last few weeks, so he planned to hunt down his family. Don was sending Lil' PJ keys back to back, and the product had the city going crazy.

***

Bad News, VA

Jazzy drove her daughter to her cousin's house so she and 50 could spend the night together on a nice dinner date in DC She'd been so busy focusing on work and on being a mommy she had no time for herself or 50. Tonight she had plans to make love to 50 and fuck his brains out.

She stopped at a red light, and an SUV truck hit her car from behind.

"What the fuck!" Jazzy shouted, as she got out of the Benz, ready to curse out whoever was in the SUV.

"You dumb ass nigga!" Jazzy yelled at the man climbing out the truck.

Boc!
Boc!
Boc!
Boc!
Boc!
Boc!

Bloody dropped her, filling her body up with bullets, then walked to her car and fired a shot into her daughter's small body. He got back in his car, pulling off, thinking about the loss of his seed, so he felt no remorse.

***

Richmond, VA
Days Later

BK posted up outside of his tire shop, on the phone with a tire company ordering a new shipment of tires. A black Ford truck pulled up and parked in front of him. He got off his phone and saw Brooke get out looking beautiful. She recently told him she had a couple of losses in her family, so she needed time to think clearly and get her mind right.

"Hey you," BK said, hugging her tightly, smelling her strong scent.

"What's up, how are you?"

"I'm ok, I'm sorry about your loss, but I'm here for you," he said.

"Thank you."

"What you doing here?"

"I'm just coming to check on you and see what you doing," she stated, needing comfort.

"Come in, I just ordered some Chinese food."

"Ok, cool," she said, following him. Then out of the blue, gunfire erupted.

Boc!

Boc!

Boc!

Boc!

Boc!

Boc!

Brooke and BK both pulled out their weapons, firing shots at the Camaro speeding by. They both looked at each other.

"Where you get that?" Brooked asked while calling the cops.

"I'm licensed, how about you?"

"I'm licensed too. I have to go." Brooke got in her truck, pulling out the lot.

BK stood there confused, walking back into his shop wondering what the fuck just happened.

Chapter 29
Downtown BK

Don did pushups in his living room, trying to stay fit and keep his chiseled frame. Last night he sent Pookie a letter. Lil' PJ told him Pookie turned Muslim in his new spot. Being in NY made Don clear his mind and focus on what he needed to do when he touched back down in VA.

Rick stuck to his word and supplied him with good product for a low price. He and his uncle Fats hadn't spoken since their meeting that went left.

The doorbell rang and Don grabbed his gun and went to open the door shirtless. When he opened the door, he was shocked to see one of the sexiest faces he'd ever seen, but she was a ghost from the past.

"Hey, Don, you look good. You gonna let me in, nigga, damn,," Bree said looking at him in her tight designer dress and high heels.

"Bree, what the fuck do you want, and why are you in NY?" He stood at the door clutching his weapon because he didn't trust her.

It'd been a long time since he'd seen his plug. When she ran off on him, he had to hunt for a new plug to maintain, and he felt betrayed by her.

"Can I come in and explain it? Don, there is a lot you don't know," Bree told him as he let her inside.

"You want a drink? I only got Henny and D'ussé," he replied, grabbing two glasses and a bottle of Henny out the kitchen.

"Henny's good." She sat down, crossing her legs, exposing her upper thighs.

"How did you find out where I live, Bree?" Don poured her a glass of liquor and sat down, staring at her with his gun in his lap just in case she tried something.

"I'll get to that, but I'mma take it from the top. I know you are Rich's son and you used to go see him. So, when you and K came into the picture, I did my research. Y'all became an overnight success, which left many questions open. Big Bio was too dumb and blinded by money to see what was going on or what trouble lurked in front of him, but I did," she stated.

"So, you know what happened to Big Bio?" he asked, taking a sip of Henny.

"Of course, but when you killed K, your own brother, I knew that had to be Rich's doing. Me and Big Bio robbed him when he got locked up, but what can I say, it's a cold game. I don't regret it."

"Facts," Don shot back.

"I finished because he couldn't be trusted. I had eyes on him, Don, and he did a lot of wrong, but I ain't judge him."

"You had him pussy whipped," Don said.

"Just like Rich, but pussy is the downfall to a nigga's empire. Anyway, the reason why I left is because the feds were on me and I needed to relocate. I found a new plug in NY and I ended up getting married," she confirmed, showing him a big diamond ring worth a couple million.

"That's what's up," Don told her, wondering who married her shady ass.

"I been hearing a lot about you in VA doing big things, but I'm sorry to hear about your mom." She gulped the rest of her drink.

"How did you know I was here, and how did you find me in Brooklyn?" Don had been thinking this since she first walked through the door.

"You're not too bright, I see."

"What you mean by that?" he shot back.

"I'm married to Rick," she said as Don almost choked on his cognac.

"Hold the fuck up, you married to my grandfather, but you fucked his son and grandson?" Don couldn't believe it.

"Yeah. Sometimes a bitch gotta use what she got to get what she want," she replied with no shame.

"That pussy must be fire."

"You have no clue, but I knew your grandfather first. He paid me to set Rich up, but I couldn't do it. My mind was still young and immature."

"Damn," he said to himself.

"Don, I need you. I got a plan and I need you to be down with me. It will be very beneficial for the both of us. Don't reply now, give it some thought, and I'll be around. But word to the wise, Don, stay away from Fats. Men like that envy their own shadows," Bree told him before leaving.

***

Stafford, VA

Capo's baby mother, Unique, walked around the small flea market buying some things for her new house. She had dark African skin with long hair and a thick body. She danced at clubs in DC for the last two years, even though Capo gave her money every week for her and their son. They hadn't been a couple or in a sexual relationship in years.

She recently saw him with a cute younger woman with exotic looks, and she couldn't front like she wasn't jealous. After shopping, she pushed the baby stroller into the car lot, seeing her son sleeping peacefully. A man followed her to her car.

"You need some help, shawty?" a man asked behind her.

"Huh?"

"You need help?"

"Nah, I'm straight," she said.

"Ok." He pulled out a blade and stabbed her in her neck ten times. Jeezy then slit the baby's neck while he was sleep before running off.

BK and two of his shooters watched Jeezy just stab Capo's baby mother. He had plans to kidnap Unique and have her bring Capo to him. Since his spots had been robbed, he did his own research to find out Capo and his crew were responsible.

"We need to find out who them niggas is, son, because they could be useful. We gunning for the same niggas," BK told one of the shooters in the front as they pulled off.

Chapter 30
Hampton, VA

Tiny knocked twice on the front door, waiting for the dope boys to open the door. Two fat niggas let her inside because she was a regular at the spot. She needed her morning hit of dog food or she was gonna be sick, and that was a big no.

Being Twin's baby mother held weight in Hampton to most drug dealers, because she would use his name when she needed dope and had no money.

"Tiny, how much you got? It's too early for your bull-shit," Sam said, knowing Tiny loved to play games.

"Ten dollars." She pulled out a ten-dollar bill.

"Here." Sam handed her one small bag of dope.

"One?"

"Yeah, you paid for one." Sam saw the look on her face and knew she wasn't jacking it.

"Sam, I spend good money every day, don't be like this," Tiny told the fat man.

"Tiny, why you always do this shit?" Sam gave her another bag of dope.

"Are you serious? I need a whole bundle, Sam."

"Shit, you know what you gotta do," he said, hoping she would be down to give him some fire head.

"You make me sick. Come upstairs so I can suck your nasty dick, and you better not nut in my mouth this time, Sam. I'm not playing," she shouted, going upstairs.

"Hold down the trap," Sam told his cousin as he went upstairs and let Tiny do her thing.

Tiny's head game was like no other. She'd make a nigga fall in love with her, until she robbed a nigga for her next fix.

***

Bad News, VA

Lil' PJ, Capo, and 50 were all chilling in a pool hall drinking and showing Capo comfort after he lost his baby mother, whom he ain't give a fuck about. Losing his son hit home for him, though. He couldn't sleep without crying or being emotionally frustrated.

Lil' Two did her best to help him and comfort her man. She was falling deep in love with him, but that wasn't enough. Hanging out with his boys did a lot for him. It didn't cover up the pain, but it cleared his mind.

"Yo, I know a nigga from Hampton who knows Twin's baby mother, so we gonna pull up on her soon," Lil' PJ said to his boys.

"Aight, I'm down, but I need like a hundred keys before the week out, bruh," 50 told Lil' PJ, holding his pool stick, looking at the new RIP Jazzy tattoo he got on his forearm yesterday.

"I got you. Capo, you need some more weight, or you good, dawg?" Lil' PJ asked, shooting his turn.

"Nah, I'm good," Capo stated flatly, drinking gin straight with no chaser or ice in his cup.

"We need to find a location on this Bloody, Jeezy, BK, and Twin nigga. I'm sick of playing cat and mouse," Lil' PJ stated.

"Tank Brim and Lil' Two on that BK nigga now, and everybody else we just waiting for a good timing." 50 didn't have a master plan and he knew they didn't either, so he had no choice but to take it day by day.

"I'mma do my own homework on these niggas, watch me," Capo said, leaving the pool hall.

Lil' PJ and 50 just shrugged their shoulders and continued to play pool. They knew Capo was hurting and venting, so they let him do him.

***

Richmond, VA

Brooke's legs were spread open like a letter V as BK grinded inside her wetness.

"Oh, oh, oh, yes," Brooke moaned while he pumped in and out of her.

Brooke came to BK's crib to vent and for closure, but her pussy was really throbbing for attention, and BK was the lucky man to fulfill her needs.

"Mmmm," BK cried out because her pussy had strong grip.

"Yess, go harder, babe," she shouted, making him speed up now, pounding her little box out.

"Uggghhh, fuck…" she screamed, holding on to his waistline, feeling every inch bury into her deepness.

BK then bent her over and fucked her until she tapped out. She rode his dick hard and crazy until she came, then BK ate her out, loving her sweet taste. Round two had both of them winded and thirsty for more. The sex vibes were there.

Romell Tukes

Chapter 31
Brooklyn, NY

Ava worked at the Barclay Center in Brooklyn at a small restaurant on the second level. Her shift was almost over, and she couldn't wait to go home and get some rest. At twenty-one, she looked much older due to stress and a hard life, but she still looked beautiful. Her flawless light-brown complexion and slim frame looked good on her.

The restaurant was packed with customers as it normally was every day because of the good cornbread and soul food.

"Yo, ma, you gonna take my order?" a fat man shouted from a private booth with two other outta shape niggas.

"What?" Ava turned around with an attitude, hating rude customers.

"You going to take my order? What, you deaf or something," he shot back, making his crew laugh.

"Deaf, huh." Ava laughed and grabbed a glass of water and tossed it in the fat nigga's face.

"You bitch!" he shouted.

Ava walked off, upset, and ran into her boss.

"Ava, table four needs you to take their order," a tall man in a white shirt told her as he approached her.

"Nigga, fuck outta here. I quit, suck my dick," she told the man, walking off to grab her purse and coat.

Her boss couldn't believe what he just heard as he watched Ava walk off, because she was his best worker.

Ava went into the locker room and opened a small locker with her items inside. For weeks she'd been wanting to quit this wack ass job, so today was long overdue for her.

"Excuse me, sir, but you can't be back here." Ava saw a man walk into the room.

"Shhh…" Don pulled out a handgun with a silencer attached to it.

"Help!" she screamed once.

Psst…

Psst…

Psst…

Psst…

Don shot her in the middle of her chest. Her body flew into the wall where she collapsed and took her last breath. He took off before someone saw him. Rick told Don two nights ago that Bloody had another sister named Ava that worked at the Barclay Center. Don didn't tell him about the visit from Bree, who was Rick's wife.

***

Richmond, VA

Jeezy parked his big body Benz in front of the projects where he was getting money at. One of his workers got his shopping bags out of the car, which had bricks of dope inside.

"Let's split this shit up, bruh. I got shit to do tonight back at Bad News." Jeezy walked into the apartment building and closed the door behind him.

Capo smoked on his third blunt of loud, watching Jeezy's every move as he went inside the build. He wanted to keep tabs on Jeezy himself, so he followed him to Richmond. Lil' Two begged him to let her come, but he told her this was personal.

After he fucked Lil' Two and put her to sleep, he snuck out their crib. The couple lived together and was really starting to get serious with each other.

Capo had a Mac 11 submachine on his lap, about to get out the car so he could knock on the door and kill Jeezy. Capo knew for a fact there were only a couple of people who would kill his seed and baby's mother.

Once outside the stolen car, three gunmen ambushed him, tackling him to the floor. Capo's weapon fell a few feet away from him. When he saw who picked up his Mack11, he knew it was over.

"Take his dumb ass inside, they waiting for him," Bloody stated as his men dragged Capo inside the apartment building Jeezy went into minutes ago.

Inside the apartment, Bloody and Jeezy and two other men surrounded Capo.

"What's poppin', Loc," Jeezy said with a hammer in his hand.

"What's cracking, y'all niggas got me, bruh." Capo showed no fear and he looked at everybody.

"You a tough nigga, huh, son?" Bloody shot Capo in his penis.

"Ahhhhh…" Capo screamed in pain.

Jeezy started hitting Capo with a hammer as his goons kicked and stomped his head in for twenty minutes, until he lost so much blood he died.

Romell Tukes

Chapter 32
Bad News, VA

"I heard they killed Capo, dawg. The city about to be turned up. I think we need to fall back until shit dies down," Sean told BK in front of his bike shop.

"You scared of war?"

"Nah, I'm just focused on this bag, BK. These niggas play by a different set of rules." Sean tried to get BK to understand what he was about to get into.

"Have no worries, bro, we straight. Them fools got so much beef niggas gonna take them out eventually." BK shrugged his shoulders.

"Aight, bruh, I'm out. I gotta drop these birds off on the northside. Who you been fucking when I Facetimed you last week? I saw a bad bitch in the background. I see you doing big things." Sean knew BK always kept a nice-looking chick around, but the one he saw Sean couldn't help but ask about.

"Me and her getting serious, bro. Shawty got class and she focused." BK saw a black Tahoe pull up. The window rolled down and he pulled out his weapon.

Boc!

Boc!

Boc!

Boc!

Boc!

Bullets hit Sean's back, making him almost do a front flip on the ground as BK ducked, shooting back.

Boom!

Boom!

Boom!

BK shot at the Tahoe SUV before rushing back into his shop to get his MP5 assault rifle. The glass windows to his shop all busted out, leaving glass everywhere as the SUV pulled off.

Minutes later, the police came and chalked out Sean's body while BK told the police he didn't know Sean and he was in the back fixing something when the gunfire took place, but he didn't hear anything.

***

Hampton, VA

Tiny arrived in a dirty crack house where fiends laid all over the place getting high or nodding off. This lifestyle was what Tiny yearned for, getting high and being free.

"Ay, Tiny, I know you got sumthin'," an old man asked, scratching his forearm, which had needle marks from shooting dope.

"Yeah, I got a little taster for us." She pulled out a bag of dog food to see the old head's eyes widen like a Pitbull about to be fed.

"You got a needle?" he asked.

"No, I'll use yours," she shot back.

"Fine, but you know I got that thing," he told her.

"I know, I got it too," she replied with no shame.

"Damn, Tiny, how long have you had HIV?" he asked unaware as he pulled out his needle.

"Four years now I think."

"Girl, you running around here fucking all these dope boys, you trying to get killed." The old head got out his belt and spoon.

"I don't force them to fuck me, and I use condoms some-times," she stated, opening the bag of dog food.

They both heard gunfire, but they paid it no mind because shit always happened in the crack house. Tiny looked at the doorway to see a man standing there with a gun as the old head shot a load of powerful dope in his veins.

50 shook his head before shooting both of them in their heads before leaving the smelly, nasty crack house.

***

Virginia Beach, VA

Since Capo's death, Lil' Two had been emotional and up-set, but she knew what needed to be done. The last two weeks she'd been building with CL. She bagged him at a concert, and they'd been talking since.

Today she wore a mini skirt and heels, showing her thick-ness and beauty. She rode in the back of CL's limousine with him, drinking as he rubbed on her legs.

"What made you give in on me?" CL asked her, sipping on a glass of Remy.

"Well, I've been lonely, and I know a good man when I see one." Lil' Two placed her hands on his manhood then un-zipped his slacks as the limo drove to his home.

"That's how you feel?" CL said as she got on her knees, taking out his rod and slowly licking the tip before taking him inch by inch into her wet mouth. Lil' Two bobbed her head up and down until she felt cold steel to her head.

"Nice try, Lil' Two." CL shocked her.

She knew it was over, so she tried to bite his penis off.

"Agghhh!" he yelled before he shot her in the head.

Romell Tukes

Chapter 33
Brooklyn, NY

Don left his condo on his way to meet Rick to talk about their shipment he planned to send out to Lil' PJ tonight. The news of Capo's death took a toll on him. He couldn't believe it when 50 told him.

Next week, Don had made up his mind to go back to VA, because he had everything he needed. He came to NY for answers, and that's what he got. While Bloody was in VA killing his guys, he'd been killing Bloody's family members, but Don knew he did enough already.

Getting inside his Cadillac sedan with tints, he looked around, making sure the coast was clear. Lately he'd been extra cautious because he knew Brooklyn wasn't his turf.

Rick wanted him to meet him at a warehouse area near Bay Plaza. Driving through the dark Brooklyn streets, a police car pulled out from an alley putting its sirens on.

"What the hell." Don pulled off on the curb, putting his Glock 17 handgun in his glove compartment.

Don rolled down his window with all his papers ready for the officer.

"Good evening, Officer," Don said to the officer approaching him.

"I need you to step out the car, sir," the officer asked.

"Officer, I've done nothing and my papers are all good." Don tried to hand him his license and registration.

"Sir, step out the car." The officer got on the walkie talkie calling for backup.

"Ok, calm down." Don opened the door slowly.

Don knew the NYPD was killing blacks left and right in Brooklyn, and he hoped that this wasn't one of those events. When both of Don's feet hit the pavement, he ran off down the street as the black cop chased him. Don had a foot on the cop as he looked behind him, but he didn't see the cop coming at him from the side, running him over.

The cop car slammed Don into the ground, leaving him in serious pain with broken bones. The officers placed Don in cuffs, roughing him up before throwing him in the back of a car. Don saw four more cop cars pull up, all looking into Don's trunk. Don tried to figure out what was going on when he saw the forensic unit come and block off the streets like a crime scene just took place.

"No wonder why you ran. I would have done the same thing," one of the cops said, opening Don's door.

"I ran because I'm a fucking black man," Don shot back.

"Yeah, so I guess those two dead bodies in the trunk ain't yours neither, huh, dick head." The white cop then shut the door, walking off.

Don couldn't believe what he just heard. He thought the police were playing mind games with him until he saw two bodies being lifted out his trunk.

***

Bad News, VA

Shay did some shopping in Target shopping center for some things for her home. Everything had been going good lately for her and her boyfriend. The holidays were hard since she had no solid family to spend her time with, so she spent time with her boyfriend's family in Ohio.

After buying what she came for, she made her way to the car lot. Shay put the bags in her car, thinking about what she heard happened to Don. 50 called her last night and told her a couple of nights ago Don was arrested in NY for a couple of murders. She cried the whole night. She couldn't believe Don could be so dumb and selfish to do this to her.

Climbing in the car, she tried to start the engine but it didn't turn over. Shay got out and popped her hood, trying to see what the problem was.

"I got you," a voice said from behind.

"Thanks," she stated, raising up, turning around to see a gun at her forehead.

"You move, you will be breathing out your fucking forehead, bitch," Twin's voice had a fearful tone.

Shay just stood there in tears.

"Dial 50's number and put it on speaker."

Shay did what she was told. When 50 got on speaker, Twin took the phone.

"50, this is the price you pay for fucking with a real gangsta, homie. Eye for an eye, sister for a sister," Twin stated.

"You touch a hair on her, you fucking dead, hoe ass nigga!" 50 barked in the speaker.

"Too late."

Boom!

Boom!

Twin fired two hollow tips in Shay's forehead then hung up the cell phone, walking off thinking checkmate.

Romell Tukes

Chapter 34
Las Vegas, NV
Three Months Later

BK and Brooke stepped out the shower after a crazy sex session in the hotel master bathroom. The couple got married hours ago in a chapel a block away from their hotel.

BK proposed to Brooke on a cruise three weeks ago, and she gladly said yes because she built a strong love connection with him over the past few months. It was her idea to have a private wedding in Vegas, and BK didn't mind at all. He honestly wanted the same thing. Brooke put on her black Miu Miu dress with her Jimmy Choo heels.

"You looking sexy, ma. I might just fuck you at the blackjack table," he told her as he put on his big-face Rolex watch.

"Mmmhmm, you so nasty, babe, but how do you feel about being married now?" She still couldn't believe she tied the knot with the perfect man.

"It feels great. When I first saw you at my shop, I knew you was someone special." BK had her blushing because she felt the same.

"Are you sure about that?" she asked, looking him in the eyes.

"Facts, stop worrying, love. We are meant to be together."

"I know, I just want to make sure we feel the same." Brooke grabbed her purse and went down to the casino area and got some drinks while enjoying a game of blackjack.

The couple enjoyed the whole weekend, going out to shows, shopping, concerts, and everything Vegas had to offer. When they made it back to VA, BK had a gift for her he'd been keeping a secret for weeks. He bought her a house outside of Richmond. It was her dream house she talked about all the time. Brooke had never been so happy in her life with BK. The way he treated her made her feel like a queen.

***

FBI, Richmond

Brooke was back at work from her honeymoon, and she had so much work to catch up on. She knew her day was going to be a long one. Her boss overloaded her because she got married and he was hating. She had eight new caseloads on her desk.

She opened the brown folder on top of the stack to see a man found shot and beaten to death inside of a project apartment months ago. She read some more of the case and saw there were two witnesses who saw a group of men leave the apartment. What she read next almost made her heart stop.

One of the witnesses stated he knew of the gunman who was a blood gang member, who went by the name Jeezy. Brooke couldn't believe she saw her brother's name on a statement dealing with the death of a man named Capo. She grabbed her big purse and tossed the folder inside hoping nobody saw it before she did or Jeezy could be in bigger trouble than she thought. She knew where her brother stayed so she left the office on her way to him.

***

North Richmond, VA

Jeezy had a thick white chick bent over, fucking her raw with no condom. Shawty was bad. He bagged her at a bar near a college area days ago.

Uhmmm, shit, fuck me wit' dat black monster!" she shouted, fucking up his bed sheets.

142

"Shut up, bitch!" Jeezy yelled, pulling her long blonde hair while fucking her at a fast pace.

The door started to ring nonstop and there was banging at the door.

"Fuck," Jeezy said, hopping out the wet pussy, putting on a pair of shorts.

"Oh my fucking god, like." The white girl got upset because she couldn't get her nut off.

"Bitch, sit your ass there." He went to answer the door to his apartment.

Not too many people knew where he lived, so he weighed his options on who it could have been. Jeezy saw his sister standing there pissed off, in her work clothes with her gun holster poking out. The last time he saw Brooke was at his little brother's funeral, and they said nothing to each other.

"I have to speak to you right now," she said.

Jeezy knew it had to be serious because she never came to his crib.

"Jeezy, who's dat?" The white chick came out the back, thinking Jeezy had another bitch at the door.

"Get out." Jeezy looked at her.

"What?" The white chick couldn't believe it.

"Bitch, get out," Jeezy told her as she walked out, upset.

Brooke walked into his apartment and threw the brown folder on his living room table near two Dracos.

"What the fuck have you gotten yourself into?" she asked.

Jeezy sat down next to her and opened the folder.

"What are you talking about?"

"Read it." Her voice got stronger.

Jeezy saw Capo's dead corpse in a photo, but when he saw a witness say his name he fucked up.

"Damn."

"Damn, that's all, Jeezy. I can't clean this up," she stated.

"What does this mean?" His tone and voice started to shake.

"You got yourself in deep shit. My boss handed this case down to me, so he had to see it," she stated.

"Fuck." Jeezy leaned back.

"There is only one way you can help."

"How?" He looked at her.

"Help me, help you."

"Brooke, I'm no rat."

"You have no choice."

"Yeah, I do. Get out."

"What? I'm trying to help you!" she shouted.

"I'm not a rat," he told her before leaving.

Chapter 35
Rikers Island Jail, NY

Don's time on Rikers Island made him wish he was locked up in VA or anywhere instead of on Rickers. The gang activity in the prison had the jail turned up every day. He saw niggas get cut in their face daily. The NY niggas fucked with him heavy because he was from outta town.

He heard Brooklyn niggas talk about Bloody all day among themselves. He also heard the Bronx cats talk about his old bunky, Knight, all the time, as if he was a god in the Bronx.

"Yo, son, I think they calling your name at the CO bubble for a visit, you heard," a Queens kid named Droopy told him before walking off.

Don only had visits from his public defender, who wasn't shit. His lawyer explained to him that it would be hard to beat two bodies found in the trunk of his rental car. Don knew the bodies weren't his work because he wasn't dumb enough to ride around with two dead niggas in the trunk. He went to his visit trying to think positive.

When he stepped foot on the packed visiting room floor, the first person he saw was Bree looking like a snack.

"Don, I like your beard." Bree eyed him up and down, seeing he'd been exercising lately.

"Bree, why are you here?

"You don't want me here?" she asked with a saddened look.

"How did you even know my name to come see me?" He didn't trust her.

"You're all over the news, Don."

"What's up though?"

"I got a lawyer for you," she told him.

"Thank you, but what do I owe that to?" Don knew nothing in life came for free, especially from a woman like Bree.

"You're a close friend and I don't want to see you in jail," she stated.

"I am? I don't know if I should take that as a blessing or curse."

"Maybe both," she laughed.

They enjoyed the visit and she wished him luck.

***

Bad News, VA

Tank Brim and 50 drove around the city on bullshit looking for any ops lacking. Since Tank Brim lost Lil' Two, he wanted blood. They found her body on the side of a road with gunshot wounds to her head.

50 felt like everybody around him was dying, first Capo, his sister, and Lil' Two. With Don being locked up again, Lil' PJ paused everything, basically shutting down all their traps until he could come up with a plan.

"What's up, dawg, you ok?" 50 asked Tank Brim.

"Yeah, I'm 'bout to slide to DC later to see what popping with—" Tank Brim's words were cut short as bullets hit the car.

They were in front of an apartment complex and Twin and three shooters were shooting up the car.

Tat!
Tat!
Tat!
Tat!
Tat!

50 and Tank Brim hopped out shooting back, going back and forth in a heated gun battle.

146

Boc!
Boc!
Boc!

Tank Brim got hit once in his arm, but 50 hit two of Twin's goons in the face, killing them. 50 saw Twin run back in one of the buildings. When 50 saw he had the perfect chance to get away from the scene, he took it and helped Tank Brim in the car because he got hit badly. Before getting inside, he saw Twin come out with a big bazooka missile.

"Oh, fuck nah!" 50 shouted, getting inside the car racing down the block, swerving into different lines.

Twin shot the missile but hit a dumpster, missing his target. When Twin saw the men in the car, he got at them, hoping today he could claim victory over his ops. His sister's death lived in his head. He knew Tiny's life wasn't perfect, but she was still family.

Romell Tukes

Chapter 36
Richmond, VA
Days Later

Jeezy drove alone to meet Brooke at a restaurant on the outskirts of the city where he knew nobody would see him. In an hour, he had a meeting with Bloody across town about getting some more drugs and taking care of their appetite.

Pulling into the lot, he saw a black SUV with no license plates. Jeezy had been doing a lot of thinking, and he wasn't trying to go down for a murder beef. He considered himself a real official street nigga, but he wasn't a jail nigga. He loved life too much. He called his sister and told her to meet him here so they could talk, because he knew if anybody had his back in this world, it was Brooke.

Brooke saw Jeezy walking toward the SUV. She was happy he contacted her, because she hadn't slept since getting on the case. Her boss recently asked her about an update, but she told him she needed more time. She knew her boss had been giving her a hard time because she wouldn't give him any pussy.

"Sis, what's up." Jeezy got inside her work truck.

"I see you came to your senses," she told him.

"How can you help, and what can I do to prevent me going to jail? Because I'm not going to jail for no nigga," Jeezy stated.

"This is a serious case, but if you can tell me who was involved, I can get you off, and if you have anything else it will be useful." Brooke saw he was a little nervous, looking out into the lot.

"The kid's name was Capo from Stafford. A kid named Bloody from NY killed Capo with his goons. I saw it all," he said.

"Bloody?" she shot back, never hearing his name before, and she knew everybody who was somebody in Richmond.

"Yeah, but Capo ran with the niggas who killed Don's mommy and our little brother," he finally admitted.

"What, Jeezy, are you serious?" She wanted to cry.

"I'm sorry, but I got into some serious shit with Don, 50, Lil' PJ, and his crew. They're the reason behind all of this," Jeezy told her.

"The kingpin kid Don?"

"Yeah."

"I could never build a solid case on him or his crew," she stated, hoping he had something on Don that would link her to CL.

"There is a new nigga named BK who's moving big weight all throughout the city. I hear he's from up top or something."

"Can you set him up?" she asked.

"Bloody I can with ease, but just give me some time," he said, feeling like a snitch.

"When you ready, call me. I'll set you up with a wire so we can have everything on audio."

"I'll call you." Jeezy got out and climbed in his car, driving off.

***

Across Town
Hours Later

Jeezy walked through the back of the house where Bloody and a gang of niggas were dog fighting two large pits.

"Yoo, what's poppin', son," Bloody shouted to Jeezy as he approached the crew.

"Ain't shit, dog."

"You trying to put in a bet, fam?" Bloody asked, looking at the dogs try to kill each other while niggas screamed and shouted.

"Nah, I'm good. I'm trying to see what we gonna do about the next shipment, bruh. My people running low."

"Ok, next week we litty. Can your men wait until then?" Bloody asked.

"Yeah."

"Good, how much you need so I can put in your order, bro?" Bloody walked into the back of the house.

"I'mma check what I got left and how much I got in the stash."

"Shit, you know I got you, bro. You can get shit on the arm any moment. I got you, son." Bloody got a bottle of Henny out the kitchen cabinet.

"Say less, blood," Jeezy stated, acting nervous, and Bloody saw this but didn't say anything.

"You coming out to DC with us tonight, homie?" Bloody stated.

"Nah, I gotta head back to Bad News and check on the spots."

"Aight, fam, do you. I'm here," Bloody said, watching Jeezy leave.

Bloody felt something funny about Jeezy's energy, but he started to push it to the back of his head.

Romell Tukes

Chapter 37
Bad News, VA

BK watched Jeezy from a distance as he left Brooke's car in a dark parking lot. He knew something was real fishy about this whole thing. Lately he'd been trying to figure out what his wife had to do with a street-level hustler like Jeezy. BK knew Brooke was a cop since the day the shooting took place at the tire shop in Richmond. When he saw her calling in the shooting on her walkie talkie, he knew from that moment she was a cop. But what he didn't know was that she was an FBI agent. He never questioned her on her career at all because he wasn't that type, but he feared she would find out about his drug empire.

When Brooke's truck left, he followed Jeezy to see what else he could find out.

***

Rikers Island, NY
Five Months Later

Don just left his unit going to court with ten other inmates who looked upset, but none of them were facing serious time. Today, Don started trial. His lawyer, Mr. Nathall, told him his trial could last one to seven days. His heart had been racing for days, and he hadn't slept in weeks since he got his trial date.

Mr. Nathall was a paid lawyer he got from Bree. His lawyer seemed like he had Don's best interest in mind, so he had faith in him. Don couldn't believe everybody in his circle in VA was dying, but Shay's death hit him hard every night he thought of her.

After getting dressed in an all-white Armani suit Bree brought up to the jail for him, it was time for court. Bree sent him letters, pics, and money daily, showing support, which surprised Don, but he didn't trust her.

***

Brooklyn Supreme Court, BK
Hours Later

"We got this shit, Mr. Wilson. Sit back and let me open up with my statement. You have a good chance of walking outta here today," Don's lawyer said to him in a small private room where Don was cuffed and chained.

"What if I don't, then I just spend the rest of my life in prison?"

"No, we fight, and I already have a direct appeal motion lined up for you if worst comes to worst, but stay faithful," Mr. Nathall stated before going out to speak to the DA and judge.

Minutes later, Don was brought out for court to see a Latin judge and a white DA all staring at him.

"Sit down, kick your feet up, champ, we got this shit," he said before the judge asked everybody to rise.

Mr. Nathall's opening statement was strong, even the jury nodded their heads understanding his logic of statement. Don had no DNA on the two dead bodies, and the bodies found in his trunk were missing for over a year.

Don explained he was in VA last year. He'd only been in NY visiting family for a couple months. His lawyer used that to his advantage, stating anybody could have been the two dead bodies in his car, which was under a fake name. Since the car didn't belong to Don, how could it have been Don's bodies It could have been anyone's.

154

When the DA spoke, he went to Don's record, even bringing up how he was accused of killing his father in prison but beat the case. Mr. Miller was a 30-year-old lawyer who was working on gaining a name in his law firm. He then accused Don of coming to NY to kill, drug traffic, and corrupt the city, which had the jury's attention now.

After the lawyers and DA went back and forth for hours, they cross examined Don and two witnesses, who said they saw Don kill the two men last year, or at least he looked like the man who killed the victims.

Judge Santana sat back on his throne listening to all the evidence, and he didn't know what to think. The jury took a break and deliberated on all the newfound evidence.

Close to two hours later, they came out in front of the courtroom and told the judge they had a conclusion. They found Don guilty on all charges, which everybody found crazy because a normal trial lasted three to four days.

Don was at a loss for words as the judge stared him down, shaking his head. Within seconds, they spoke his words and gave Don 75 to life, a sentence so high he knew the only time he would see daylight was from his cell window.

Romell Tukes

Chapter 38
Bad News, VA

Bloody and his crew parked at a train station to meet with a man named BK, who reached out to him. Getting out his car, he saw BK, who looked familiar, but he knew these country niggas all looked like somebody he knew from back home.

"What's good, fam, thanks for pulling up," BK said strongly.

"You from NY?" Bloody asked.

"Facts, how about you?" BK hadn't run into too many niggas from the town in VA.

"So, what's up, bro? I don't mean to rush, but I have to go attend to some business outta town," Bloody stated.

"You know a nigga named Jeezy?" BK asked.

"Yeah, that's the homie, why?"

"I saw him with you a couple of days ago and before I break the news to you, I want to make sure," BK told him, looking at Bloody's blank expression.

"What news, fam?"

"Jeezy working with the police, fam. I been watching for a few weeks now, and he been meeting with dem boys." BK knew this was the right thing to do.

"Fuck, son, I knew this nigga was moving funny!" Bloody shouted to himself, in deep thought, feeling betrayed.

"Maybe you had to find out like this, son."

"How you know all of this?"

"My wife is a cop and he be having meetings with her. She don't know my dealings in the streets, and I plan to keep it like that for as long as possible," BK stated.

"So, you think he gonna rat on you?" Bloody asked.

"Anything is possible."

"No doubt, I'm looking into it." Bloody couldn't believe this.

"If you don't, I will." BK then walked off, getting in his car.

***

Virginia Beach, VA

CL had to pay his phone bill, so he waited in the phone store for the line to die down. He knew in a couple of hours he had a meeting with an important stockbroker he met last week at a business convention in Richmond. One thing he knew for sure was the drug game wasn't going to last forever, so he wanted to invest his money in something legit.

The dope game had been booming lately. He just had a sit down with his brother last night talking about the ops, business, and their sister who lived in D.C. and Miami. The beef with 50 and his crew had been taking up a lot of time. He thought Twin would be able to help with his resume, but he wasn't doing shit. CL had been giving him keys monthly and his ops were still running around gunning for his head.

He paid his phone bill and got back in his limousine so his driver could take him to his meeting. When he closed the door, he saw Tank Brim sitting in the back with a gun pointed at him with a 30-shot clip. Tank Brim tapped on the back door, and 50 pulled off with CL's guard slumped in the driver's seat.

"Cheers, you little niggas finally got me." CL played tough, but his heart was racing at a rapid speed.

"Any last words, dawg? You been sitting back ducked off calling shots like a boss but scared to put in work," Tank Brim told him.

"The goal is to get your money and keep your hands clean, young gent. If not, you'll remain broke." CL had a gun in his lower back, but he weighed his options.

"Time's up, playboy."

Boc!

Boc!

Boc!

Tank Brim shot him three times in his head before the limousine pulled over. 50 and Tank got out and changed cars.

Romell Tukes

Chapter 39
Sux 1 Prison, VA

Today was Pookie's birthday, and he didn't receive any mail, so he was under stress. The prison guards in the special housing unit "SHU" treated him badly, beating him with cuffs on daily. The guard would spit and piss in his drinks and put razors in his food, but Pookie always checked his food before eating it now.

Once the police found out he killed another cop at his last prison, he became their number one target and public enemy. Since becoming Muslim, he'd been focused on his deen and Islamic studies.

Pookie made a strong rope out his bed sheets and tied it to the vent. For the past few weeks, he'd been thinking about committing suicide but couldn't bring himself to do it. Today, his depression was bothering him. He'd been on meds, but the meds weren't enough to put him to sleep. Living with HIV and no chance of an appeal had him thinking he had nothing to live for.

He knew they would be doing meds soon, so he stared at the rope tied to the vent above his bed.

"Allah Akbar," he shouted before taking a chair and tying himself to his rope and hanging himself.

Within seconds he was dead and hanging from his cell vent. When the nurse walked by to give him his meds, she called other guards when she saw him lifeless.

"You have to save him," the female nurse told the officer who looked through Pookie's cell.

"Fuck him, he's already dead," the cop told her.

"Sir, I have to examine his body, or I'll get in trouble." The nurse couldn't believe what the CO was doing.

"You find you a set of keys then, because you not using mine, nigger lover." The CO walked off.

The nurse married a black man two years ago, and all the corrections officers hated her because she was a bad white chick. She went to other COs in a whole unit to help her get Pookie's body. When she made it to Pookie, he was already cold and dead. She had tears in her eyes for Pookie. She hated to see young black men lose their life. The nurse stood strong with the Black Lives Matter movement, and that's why the police hated her.

***

Wendy Prison, NY

Don hated looking at the walls all day, but he had no choice. The prison he was at had a large number of black guards, unlike other NY state prisons.

Wendy was located upstate near Buffalo and Rochester. Don met a lot of good niggas from NY in his unit he dealt with on the regular. His lawyer disappeared and luckily, Lil' PJ paid for his appeal lawyer. Don had a motion filed for his direct appeal so he could give his time back.

Don was walking through the prison's long halls on his way to a visit he had no clue about. Getting back into prison mode wasn't in his plans when he left prison the first time.

Prison in NY was way better than doing time in VA. The prison had trailer visits for married couples where inmates' wives and family could come for the weekends and chill in a mobile home on the prison compound. He could use the tablet all day, talk on the phone, use his TV and cook on his crock pot.

50 told him last night Pookie killed himself a few weeks ago in his cell. At first Don thought the police did it because

he knew the police killed inmates daily and told their loved ones they killed themselves due to mental issues and prison stress.

Rick saw Don come out in green state pants and a white designer collar shirt.

"OG, what's up." Don sat down across from his grandpop.

"I see you hold water well, unlike Rich, but I'mma do whatever it takes to get you home. I paid for your appeal lawyer, so hopefully you'll be home soon. Just put your faith in God."

"I always do."

"Somebody had to set you up, kid. I know you not that dumb, and the two men that were killed and found in your trunk were two drug dealers."

"How you know?"

"Because they worked for me, Don, that's how I knew this was a setup," Rick stated, looking at Don reading him, something he'd practiced for years.

"I wonder who would try to set me up. I don't know nobody," Don stated, confused.

"I'mma find out who did this, just do your time and stay focused. Hit them weights and them books and stay focused on knowledge so you can come out to be more successful." Rick knew about prison even though he never did a day in prison.

"I know how to do time, old head. I do day for day," Don said.

"I hear you, my G, but I gotta go." Rick looked at the clock on the wall.

"You drove eight hours to see me?"

"Hell no, I took my private jet to Rochester to meet with an old friend, then stopped by here to make sure you doing good."

"Thanks."

"Sure, call me." Rick got up to leave.

Chapter 40
Bad News, VA

Bloody called Jeezy out to a small bar his soldier girl owned. The bar had a front and back. The back had a pool table, TV area, juke box, and a stage for rap artists to perform every Friday night. Six of Bloody's goons hung out and smoked blunts of mid-grade weed and drank bottles of Cîroc.

Since meeting with BK, there was no doubt in Bloody's mind that Jeezy had some fishy shit going on. His main focus at the moment was getting his ops out the way, but Jeezy fucked up his plans.

Jeezy got out his trunk and made his way into the bar to see three black trucks.

"Hey, Jeezy, what's up, where you been?" Linda asked, cleaning the bar counter.

"I been laying low, Linda. You know how I do. How's the baby?" he asked the wife of his boy, Rell.

"He's good, doing what kids do, but I'm trying to lose this baby fat. Rell gonna pay to get my body done next week. I can't wait," she boasted.

"I bet."

"All the guys in the back." She walked off, strutting her big ass.

Jeezy wondered what Bloody wanted, because he spoke to him yesterday and he told Jeezy he was going outta town for a week.

"What's poppin', five." Jeezy embraced Bloody, but the hug was kinda weak.

"Ain't shit, just wanted to call you so you can chop it up with the homies and me before we slide to Miami." Bloody sat on a stool.

"I thought you left yesterday, bruh." Jeezy looked around to see the homies all looking at him oddly.

"You thought wrong, but since you asking questions, I got a couple of my own, fam," Bloody said as all six goons now surrounded Jeezy in a circle.

"What's going on, dawg?" Jeezy got nervous, backing into a wall.

"Niggas saying you working with dem people." Bloody got up, pulling his gun out, and his men did the same thing.

"You tripping." Jeezy knew he fucked up and Bloody got on to him.

"Nah, son, you wilding... Put him on the pool table," Bloody told his men, and they all grabbed Jeezy.

When Jeezy tried to fight them off, they started beating the shit outta him. One of the men crushed a Cîroc bottle over his head, knocking him clean out.

Seconds later, Jeezy woke up on the pool table stretched out like Jesus, with his legs and arms tied tightly to the edges. He saw a rat hanging over his face tied to a thin rope, hanging from a ceiling light.

"You rat ass bitch. What you tell them people, fam?" Bloody stood next to him with a long blade, tracing it down his stomach.

"I told on 50 and BK. I didn't tell on you, bruh, that's on the gang," Jeezy cried, feeling the rat take a shit on his face as the goons laughed.

"Who was you working with?"

"My sister, Brooke, she's an FBI agent, dawg. You don't gotta do this, bro," Jeezy cried out loud.

"Aight, boy," Bloody said before cutting Jeezy's eyeballs out and his tongue out his mouth.

***

Hampton, VA

Twin drove around the city in his muscle car he recently bought to get low in. He'd been switching up his cars daily because 50 and his crew had been going back and forth in Bad News and Hampton for the past few weeks. He still had his foot on Bloody's neck, working with him and getting keys of dope for the low.

Since CL got killed, his traps had been slowing down, but Bloody had been pushing his shit for the low. Twin pulled into the car wash to give his car a clean look because it was dirty. Putting his car through the wash tunnel, he put his car on neutral. After going through the rinse and spin cycle, the gang of workers hand dried his car.

An SUV pulled up, and a man with an AR-15 assault rifle got out and sprayed Twin's car with bullets, killing him and the group of car wash workers. The masked man, who was 50, climbed back in the SUV, racing off back to Bad News.

Romell Tukes

Chapter 41
Norfolk State University, VA

Tank Brim got done fucking Chavonne doggy style in her dorm room.

"Baby, you got my pussy hurting," she said, laying there unable to move after catching her fourth nut.

"You got that knockout, shawty. I can't lie, you about to have a nigga marry that pussy, shawdy," Tank Brim laughed.

"Stop lying, nigga."

"Nah, baby girl, I need that wet, wet, you feel me, shawdy," Tank Brim told her, placing a finger into her wet, drenched coochie.

"My roommate out there fucking her new boo on the couch. She be having the whole living room stanking." Chavonne hated even using the bathroom after her roommate. Her pussy smelled so bad.

"I gotta go. I hope I'll be able to slide out. I'm not trying to cock block them," Tank Brim said, getting dressed.

"You should be good. I'll go with you." She got up naked, putting on a robe to go with him.

When she opened the door, she couldn't believe what was on the other side of the door.

"Get your dirty ass back in there, bitch, before I blow your brains out," Bloody told her, kicking her to the floor.

Tank Brim reached for his weapon, and Bloody shot him in the shoulder.

Boc!

"Ahhhaaahhhh, bitch nigga," Tank Brim cried in pain.

Chavonne tried to turn around and crawl away.

Boc!
Boc!
Boc!

The bullets entered her back, killing her instantly.

"Let's get down to business, champ. Where can I find 50 or Lil' PJ?"

"Fuck you, hoe," Tank Brim shot back, sticking to the G code he always lived by in the streets, keeping his mouth shut.

"Y'all VA niggas real tough." Bloody then shot him twice in his head, killing him.

Bloody choked Chavonne's roommate out minutes ago, leaving her dead body on the couch as if she was sleep. He met her at a bar days ago, and she started telling him how her roommate was fucking with some blood nigga named Tank and she disliked him. That was Bloody's door opener, so he'd been lurking around the college campus to catch him lacking.

***

Bad News, VA

50 heard rumors about Tank Brim being murdered hours ago on a college campus, and he couldn't believe it. He called Tank Brim's auntie to ask her if she heard the news or if it was just a myth. He'd been calling Tank Brim's phone all day to only get the voicemail. He did know Tank was going to chill with one of his side bitches.

When Tank Brim's auntie picked up the phone, he could hear the older woman's cries.

"Baby, my nephew is gone, they killed him," she cried into the phone.

"Damn… I'm so sorry, Aunty. If there is anything I can do, let me know," 50 told her, holding back his own tears for the last of his best friends.

"Ok, baby, be safe and take care of yourself." The woman then hung up so she could grieve over her nephew's murder.

***

Clinton Prison, NY
One Month Later

Don walked to the legal mail room to get his mail. Prison was prison for Don. He'd been on his legal work and exercising, trying his best to stay out the way. He had two niggas he fucked with on the regular in his unit from Yonkers, NY. He did everything with them.

The line for the legal mail was a little long, so he waited patiently until it was his turn.

"Mr. Wilson," a CO called Don's last name.

"That's me," Don stated.

"Open it in front of me and sign here," the CO said, waiting for his shift to end.

"Thank you." Don walked off, passing inmates.

Don started to read his legal mail, which was from the government telling him they received his direct appeal. He knew his appeal lawyer was now doing his job, so he was happy about that.

Walking back to his cell, he prayed the government would overturn his case. His appeal lawyer told him he found ten strong grounds for an appeal and he had a strong fight.

Romell Tukes

Chapter 42
Richmond, VA

Agent Brooke had a long day dealing with her brother's funeral and a busy day at work in the office. Two weeks ago, when she received the call about Jeezy's death, she rushed to the scene and couldn't believe what awaited her.

Seeing her brother tied to a pool table with his eyes and tongue cut out, she cried that whole day. Jeezy had to have a closed casket funeral service because his face was too gruesome for the public. Brooke felt like it was her fault he was dead, for pushing him into a corner where he wouldn't return. Days before his death, he told her Bloody and his own homies were moving funny. She told him don't worry about it, that she could prevent it from the gate, but she let her career overthink her better judgment. She drove back home to her husband, Kirk, who treated her like a queen every day.

Brooke thought good men were all dead or disappeared from the face of the earth, but that wasn't the case with Kirk. He was everything and more any female would want in a husband and best friend.

Lately he'd been acting funny, but she knew she was hard to put up with, but tonight she planned to fuck him good and suck his dick so good he would beg her to stop.

Pulling into her driveway, she parked next to the Benz and the motorcycle. Walking into her home, she smelled candles burning, she heard old school R&B, and she smelled curry chicken.

"Hi, baby." Brooke walked into the kitchen and saw her husband cooking and dancing.

"What's up, boo. I know you had a long day, so I just want to show support," her husband said.

"Ohhh, I love you." She kissed him.

173

"I got a warm bubble bath running upstairs for you, baby," he told her, turning down the stove fire.

"Ok, I'mma go take a bath real quick, you're welcome to join me." She left smiling, hoping he was down to get freaky.

She left her purse and coat on the living room couch and went to bathe. She got undressed and got out in the tub. Luckily, the water was still hot when she got inside. Seconds later, Kirk came into the bathroom with an FBI badge and a gun in his hand, which was hers.

"Kirk, what are you doing?" she asked on alert.

"Agent Brooke," he said, shaking his head. "Why couldn't you just mind your business?" he said, sitting on the edge of the tub with her gun pointing at her.

"Kirk, you're starting to scare me." She feared for her life now.

"You should have not been so thirsty to build a case on me."

"On you? I don't know what you saying, Kirk, this must be a mistake. I'm an FBI agent. I should've told you, but I didn't want you to judge me," she said.

"Brooke, how slow can you be? I'm BK. The one you had your rat ass brother try to investigate." BK's real name was Kirk, but in NY he went by the name Official.

"Kirk, I thought you loved me. You don't have to do this, please. I can make this go away, Kirk, I promise," she cried.

"I know you can, but I'mma kill you then make it look like you did it yourself, and head back to NY. My job is done here." BK lifted the gun.

Boc!
Boc!
Boc!
Boc!
Boc!

174

Bullets hit Agent Brooke in her face, killing her. He cleaned the gun with a towel and took Brooke's hand, placing her fingerprints all over the gun to make it look like a suicide crime scene instead of murder.

BK took all the evidence out of the house to make it look like she lived by herself. Since they were married, he knew the police would contact him and tell him about her suicide, and he had his story ready.

Two days later, a team of FBI agents arrived at his place of business to ask him questions and inform him his wife had committed suicide. BK acted surprised, and he went as far as crying in front of the men and his employees. He told them he hadn't seen her in days, and they didn't live together because Brooke was going through a serious stage of depression due to the loss of her family members.

When the FBI left, BK went for the airport, leaving his crew with a ton of bricks and his two shops.

Romell Tukes

Chapter 43
Bad News, VA

Lil' PJ walked out the trap house at the back door with two big bags filled with money. His luxury car was parked in a back alley near another trap house they ran molly and pounds of weed out of. Placing the bags in his seat, he jumped in the driver seat, pulling off in a rush.

In the back seat, he had eight big bags full of money and drugs. Lil' PJ had been riding around all day collecting all the money and drugs from his stash houses and traps. He made sure he was unseen so nobody could put his face on the robberies he just committed. He basically robbed himself and Don. Five of his workers were blowing up his phone to tell him niggas robbed his spots, but Lil' PJ didn't plan on answering.

The BMW made it to the expressway, doing 80 mph on his way to New York where he had a crew already stationed waiting on him. Lil' PJ felt like he deserved his own empire instead of running behind Don all day. With Don being locked up in NY, he knew it was now or never to rob Don of everything he helped build.

Lil' PJ knew most niggas would consider what he just did a double cross, but he felt like he earned everything he just took. Every time Don was in prison, Lil' PJ put his blood, sweat, and tears into the streets by himself. He had a cousin in NY, so he planned to set up shop out there and run it up, then go to Tennessee.

One thing he knew for sure was his relationship with Don after this was in a rocky place, but Lil' PJ didn't care. He was ready for whatever. The black BMW hit I-85 North, as Lil' PJ listened to Future's new album, in his zone with a Draco on the passenger seat.

***

Bad News, VA
Next Day

50 couldn't believe what his crew told him.

"How the fuck nobody see a nigga or crew rob four spots?" 50 asked a crew of young dope dealers standing on the front porch of one of their traps that got robbed last night.

"We all went out, 50, for Rush's birthday party," one of them spoke up, hoping 50 didn't think he had any parts of this.

"There wasn't a soul here, you telling me?" 50 asked.

"Nah, bruh," one of his workers said.

"Hold on, Lil' OP said he saw a black BMW speed off down the block," Vok said, coming out the screen door.

"A black BMW, you sure?" 50 thought about the only nigga who had a black BMW in the hood.

"Yeah, bruh, we been blowing up Lil' PJ's phone, but his shit went to voicemail, bruh. You the only one who picked up," Vok told his boss.

"Aight, y'all niggas lay low, dawg, until I figure this shit out." 50 left, calling Lil' PJ, only to get his voice mail also.

50 hoped Lil' PJ was safe and still alive, because everybody around him had been dying back to back. Tank Brim's death hit home for him, so now he rolled around in an SUV with three shooters. Since killing Twin, he could put his focus on Bloody because he was his main target and threat. What he didn't understand was how a black BMW left the scene around the same time the spots were robbed. The only nigga in the city who had that type of car was Lil' PJ, and that's what 50 found odd.

His goons drove through the city, but 50 planned to stop at a chick's crib who he saw with Lil' PJ weeks ago at his projects.

***

Across Town

50 got out the truck and saw a couple of niggas posted up in the projects, doing nothing.

"Yo, where Angie live at, High?" 50 asked a nigga he went to school with.

"What's up, 50, shawdy live in apartment 5B in the back complex." High pointed to the back.

"Aight, bruh, tell Rake I said what up," 50 said before walking to Angie.

When he knocked on Angie's door, she opened it, wearing denim shorts and a tank top. She was a decent looking black chick with a banging body, and word was her sex game drove a nigga to suicide not once but twice.

"Hey, 50, what a surprise." She smiled, licking her lips because she always liked his swag and wanted to see what his pipe game was hitting on.

"What's up, Angie, I got a question," he asked.

"Anything," she stated.

"Have you seen Lil' PJ?"

"Nah, not in a few days, but last time I spoke to him he was acting real funny," she stated.

"Oh yeah, he ain't say nothing like where he was going?"

"Noo...oh yeah, he said he was going out to NY and it was his time to turn up. But that was pillow talk, you know how I do. I give a nigga some of this wetness, he go crazy, start telling me about how many bodies he got and who he ratted on and shit." Angie saw him turn to leave. She didn't even get the chance to invite him in so she could put her head game on him.

Chapter 44
Brooklyn, NY

BK loved the feeling of being back home in NY where he was from. He went by the name Official in NY, but when he went outta town niggas called him BK. He went to VA and opened two legit businesses and set up shop to move drugs. Finding a plug was one of his main goals while in VA, but he had a steady plug in NY.

When he saw the Rolls Royce headlights pull into the parking lot of a closed dance studio, he got out his car.

"Girl, you looking younger and younger every day, I swear." Official hugged his connect.

"Official, you know all the right shit to say, but how was your trip? I see you back a little early," she stated, thinking he would have been in VA for at least a year or so opening shop.

"Nah, I ran into a little problem, so I'll be back home for a while until we come up with another city to take over," he told her, looking at her big breasts.

"What happened? That city is a gold mine. I hope you didn't fuck this up," she sounded upset.

"I had to kill an FBI agent, but we set up shop, ma don't worry about that, you heard," he told her.

"Ok, good."

"What's been going on up here? I been missing in action," he said.

"Well, soon I'mma make my move, so be ready." The woman was Bree, and she and Official been cool since she came to NY.

She met him fresh from home and put him on to a big bag. His name was heavy in Brooklyn, so she wanted him on her team. Official used to work for Fats years ago, until shit went sour.

"I'm out, call me," Official told Bree.

"You going to visit your bm?" Bree asked with a chuckle.

"Hahaha." He knew she was being funny because his bm burned him before he went to VA, but she's the one who took him to the hospital.

"Bye, Official." Bree got back into the Wraith, pulling off.

***

Richmond, VA
FBI Building

Agent Rayovaco looked over his fellow partner's and agent's unsolved murder, trying to figure it out because he felt like pieces were missing. Her death shocked the whole building because she had a bright future and she worked her ass off. When he went to go speak with her husband, Kirk, he felt there was something off about him. Agent Rayovaco saw a lot of people in grief when their loved ones died, and Kirk's sadness was too fake. He was doing too much. He made plans to go by and see Kirk again to retrace the storyline to see if there were any loopholes.

Recently he found out Jeezy was Brooke's brother, which he couldn't believe at all. Looking into Jeezy's case and the way he died, there had to be a lot more behind what he was seeing. He pulled up Jeezy's background and saw he was involved in a recent murder case. He wondered why she was holding back this type of info. He knew this could be something bigger than what he thought.

***

Clifton Prison, NY
Three Months Later

182

Don sat in his cell stressed out but trying to remain strong and positive. Today he had a legal call, and what his appeal lawyer told him almost made him shed a tear. His direct appeal was shot down. He lost his chance of going home soon.

Now Don had to wait to file another appeal, but that could take up to a year. He didn't know what to do or think right now. His life was at a pause.

Lil' PJ was gone, and 50 claimed Lil' PJ robbed them, but Don found that hard to believe because Lil' PJ was like a brother to him. He took a nap, trying to sleep away his stress.

Romell Tukes

Chapter 45
Bad News, VA

Bloody and two of his men walked in a neighborhood store to grab a box of Dutch masters and a six pack of beer. Nightfall covered the city as rain poured down.

"Yo, where the 211-steel reserve?" Bloody asked the store clerk, who looked at his all-red attire, disgusted because he was a church pastor.

"In the back, hoodlum," the clerk said, showing no fear seeing Bloody's gun poking out his waistband.

"Play yourself if you want, fam," Bloody told him before walking off.

"Punk," the clerk mumbled under his breath when Bloody walked off.

After paying for everything, Bloody walked out the store, putting his hoodie over his head because the rain was coming down hard. Twenty men had guns all pointed at Bloody and his crew in front of the store.

"You don't look so happy," 50 said, walking through the crowd with his Tommy gun.

"Regardless, I'm up, fam. I came to your town, killed your mom and your little crew, so I'm ready to die." Bloody looked 50 in his eyes.

"Respect."

Tat!
Tat!
Tat!
Tat!
Tat!
Tat!
Tat!
Tat!

Tat!

Tat!

50 killed Bloody and his two shooters. 50's crew wanted some action but like always, 50 wanted to be the star of the movie.

"Leave these bum ass niggas here, bruh," 50 told his niggas from his projects he grew up with.

The store clerk came outside to see three dead bodies outside of his store. At first, he panicked, until he saw who it was.

"May God bless their young, lost souls," the clerk said as a young hooker came out the back.

"What happened...oh my god!" she screamed, seeing Bloody and his crew laid out dead.

"Let's go inside, we ain't see shit, you hear me. Now come suck this dick real quick." He slapped her small ass.

Minutes later, five trucks and two cars pulled inside 50's projects as he and his crew chilled in the parking lot as the rain stopped.

"What the fuck is this?" 50 said before a gang of federal agents hopped out in combat gear.

"FBI!" Agent Rayovac yelled, leading the fourteen-man crew. They were in 50's hood to arrest him and his crew. They saw them kill Bloody less than twenty minutes ago. He was building a case on 50 and Bloody. When he watched 50 and his crew surround Bloody, he called his boss and he gave him the green light. 50's little homie shot first, and all mayhem broke loose in the parking lot.

Boom!

Boom!

Boom!

The agents shot two of 50's goons as the parking lot turned into World War III.

Boc!

186

Boc!
Tat!
Tat!
Tat!
Tat!

50 shot Agent Rayovaco in his face, killing him before another shot his boy next to him trying to cover him. There was a building next to him where he could make it to the front of his projects and escape.

50's crew and the feds continued to engage in a vicious shootout as 50 snuck off through his projects.

***

Manhattan, NY

Bree and Rick had been having sex all night, and Rick was now laying in their condo snoring loud. She got out of bed and put on her Versace robe, walking into the master bathroom connected to the bedroom. She grabbed a Glock 32 handgun from under the sink that she planted there days ago. Tonight would be the night that would change her life forever.

"Nigga, wake your hoe ass up." She slapped him with the butt of the pistol so hard she busted his forehead.

"Bitch, what the fuck is wrong with you?" Rick sat up, feeling the blood pour from his forehead.

"You know what, Rick, I regret not killing you a while back." She pointed her gun at him.

"You ungrateful little bitch!" Rick couldn't believe this was happening after all he did for Bree. He showed her the game, now it was backfiring.

"I'm a little ungrateful bitch, but I'm about to be a richer bitch," she boasted with her gun trained on him.

"Whatever you want, Bree, you can have. You don't have to do this." Rick stopped the blood from dripping into his eyes.

"Rick, this is not up for debate. I put up with your bullshit long enough, now it's time I get what I deserve. I'm sorry, love." Bree saw his lips move, but nothing came out.

Boc!
Boc!
Boc!
Boc!
Boc!
Boc!
Boc!
Boc!

Bree shot Rick all in his chest and watched him die slowly. The condo walls were soundproof, so she wasn't too worried about the neighbors. She had all Rick's safe numbers and bank accounts. She was his wife, so she had access to all of that. Official and his boy, Bones, were on their way to clean up her mess, but her ride was outside waiting on her.

Outside, Bree got in the passenger seat of a new model Acura with tints that had been waiting on her for two hours.

"What's up, cousin, you ready to get rich?" Bree asked her cousin.

"Hell yeah!" Lil' PJ said, pulling out of his parking spot, feeling his hand itch.

Lil' PJ and Bree were cousins, and they recently found each other months ago. When Bree reached out to him with her master plan, he was all in for it, but at first, he wasn't too sure about crossing his best friend.

They drove to Lil' PJ's hotel so Bree could go over their plan again.

"You got all the money and drugs in there?" Bree asked, walking into the hotel room in the hood of Brooklyn.

"Of course." Lil' PJ opened the hotel door, walking inside.

Lil' PJ robbed 50 and came to NY to open shop, then he planned to go to Tennessee and do his thing down there.

"I can't wait to open up shop in Cashville," Lil' PJ said, walking to the bathroom to get all the duffle bags out of the sink cabinet.

When he walked back into the living room, Bree stood there with a gun pointed at him.

"You know what I hate, Lil' PJ?" she asked, moving closer.

"What?"

"A snake who snakes real niggas," she replied.

"Shit, bitch, you a snake," Lil' PJ shot back, because this was all her idea.

"Yeah, but I'm a snake that bit for a better situation, you just a snake looking for a victim, and this ain't that, playa."

Boc!

Boc!

Boc!

Boc!

Lil' PJ's body hit the floor, making a loud thump. Bree stood over him, seeing he was still alive, and fired a shot in his head, now killing him. She grabbed all the bags, thinking what a nigga would do for clout. Bree didn't care about him being family, she just met him, and she heard he robbed one of her spots years ago. She told him a fake name, so she wouldn't expose her hand, because if he found out she was Bree, he would have been on alert.

***

Manhattan, NY
Days Later

Mr. Nathall walked outta his office building on his way home from a long day at work. On his way to his SUV, a group of gunmen jumped out an alley and snatched him up, dragging him into a dark alley.

Fats was leaning on a Maybach sedan, smoking a blunt of strong loud named Pink Runtz.

"Mr. Nathall, you went against our agreement," Fats stated.

"I fulfilled our deal. The kid got life in prison!" he shouted with fear.

"Don got an appeal in the court." Fats blew smoke out his mouth, walking toward the lawyer.

"Fats, I did what you asked of me, please." Mr. Nathall's body started to tremble as Fats' goons held him by his arms.

"No, I wanted him to not have any type of chance of an appeal."

"Everybody has a shot of an appeal. I can't prevent that," the lawyer said.

"Yes, you could have."

"Let me make it right."

"It's too late." Fats pulled out a gun from his lower back.

Boc!

Boc!

Boc!

Boc!

Boc!

Boc!

Fats walked back to his car and got in the back on his way to Queens, to see Rick's old traps he took over since his death. When his dad, Rick, died, he threw a party and took over all his spots he used to sell drugs at.

Fats didn't bother touching Brooklyn because he didn't want the headache. He was the one who put the two bodies in

Don's trunk to set him up for killing Rich, his brother. Fats prayed Don never got out of prison, or it could be a big problem…

To Be Continued in Jack Boyz vs. Dope Boyz

Romell Tukes

Lock Down Publications and Ca$h Presents assisted publishing packages.

BASIC PACKAGE $499
Editing
Cover Design
Formatting

UPGRADED PACKAGE $800
Typing
Editing
Cover Design
Formatting

ADVANCE PACKAGE $1,200
Typing
Editing
Cover Design
Formatting
Copyright registration
Proofreading
Upload book to Amazon

LDP SUPREME PACKAGE $1,500
Typing
Editing
Cover Design
Formatting
Copyright registration
Proofreading
Set up Amazon account
Upload book to Amazon

Advertise on LDP Amazon and Facebook
page

***Other services available upon request.
Additional charges may apply
Lock Down Publications
P.O. Box 944
Stockbridge, GA 30281-9998
Phone # 470 303-9761

Submission Guideline

Submit the first three chapters of your completed manuscript to ldpsubmissions@gmail.com, subject line: Your book's title. The manuscript must be in a .doc file and sent as an attachment. Document should be in Times New Roman, double spaced and in size 12 font. Also, provide your synopsis and full contact information. If sending multiple submissions, they must each be in a separate email.

Have a story but no way to send it electronically? You can still submit to LDP/Ca$h Presents. Send in the first three chapters, written or typed, of your completed manuscript to:

LDP: Submissions Dept
Po Box 944
Stockbridge, Ga 30281

DO NOT send original manuscript. Must be a duplicate.

Provide your synopsis and a cover letter containing your full contact information.

Thanks for considering LDP and Ca$h Presents.

NEW RELEASES

COKE KINGS 5 by T.J. EDWARDS
MONEY GAME 2 by SMOOVE DOLLA
LOYAL TO THE SOIL by JIBRIL WILLIAMS
A GANGSTA'S PAIN by J-BLUNT
MONEY IN THE GRAVE 2 by MARTELL "TROU-
BLESOME" BOLDEN
THE BRICK MAN 2 by KING RIO
A DOPEBOY'S DREAM 3 by ROMELL TUKES

Coming Soon from Lock Down Publications/Ca$h Presents

BLOOD OF A BOSS **VI**

SHADOWS OF THE GAME II

TRAP BASTARD II

By **Askari**

LOYAL TO THE GAME **IV**

By **T.J. & Jelissa**

IF TRUE SAVAGE **VIII**

MIDNIGHT CARTEL IV

DOPE BOY MAGIC IV

CITY OF KINGZ III

NIGHTMARE ON SILENT AVE II

By **Chris Green**

BLAST FOR ME **III**

A SAVAGE DOPEBOY III

CUTTHROAT MAFIA III

DUFFLE BAG CARTEL VII

HEARTLESS GOON VI

By **Ghost**

A HUSTLER'S DECEIT III

KILL ZONE II

BAE BELONGS TO ME III

By **Aryanna**

KING OF THE TRAP III

By **T.J. Edwards**

GORILLAZ IN THE BAY V

3X KRAZY III

STRAIGHT BEAST MODE II
De'Kari
KINGPIN KILLAZ IV
STREET KINGS III
PAID IN BLOOD III
CARTEL KILLAZ IV
DOPE GODS III
Hood Rich
SINS OF A HUSTLA II
ASAD
RICH $AVAGE II
MONEY IN THE GRAVE II
By Martell Troublesome Bolden
YAYO V
Bred in the Game 2
S. Allen
CREAM III
By Yolanda Moore
SON OF A DOPE FIEND III
HEAVEN GOT A GHETTO II
By Renta
LOYALTY AIN'T PROMISED III
By Keith Williams
I'M NOTHING WITHOUT HIS LOVE II
SINS OF A THUG II
TO THE THUG I LOVED BEFORE II
By Monet Dragun

Romell Tukes

QUIET MONEY IV

EXTENDED CLIP III

THUG LIFE IV

By **Trai'Quan**

THE STREETS MADE ME IV

By **Larry D. Wright**

IF YOU CROSS ME ONCE II

By **Anthony Fields**

THE STREETS WILL NEVER CLOSE II

By K'ajji

HARD AND RUTHLESS III

THE BILLIONAIRE BENTLEYS II

Von Diesel

KILLA KOUNTY II

By Khufu

MONEY GAME III

By Smoove Dolla

A GANGSTA'S KARMA II

By FLAME

JACK BOYZ VERSUS DOPE BOYZ

By Romell Tukes

MURDA WAS THE CASE II

Elijah R. Freeman

THE STREETS NEVER LET GO II

By Robert Baptiste

AN UNFORESEEN LOVE III

By **Meesha**

198

KING OF THE TRENCHES II
by **GHOST & TRANAY ADAMS**

MONEY MAFIA II

LOYAL TO THE SOIL II

By **Jibril Williams**

QUEEN OF THE ZOO II

By **Black Migo**

THE BRICK MAN III

By King Rio

VICIOUS LOYALTY II

By Kingpen

A GANGSTA'S PAIN II

By J-Blunt

Available Now

RESTRAINING ORDER **I & II**

By **CA$H & Coffee**

LOVE KNOWS NO BOUNDARIES **I II & III**

By **Coffee**

RAISED AS A GOON I, II, III & IV

BRED BY THE SLUMS I, II, III

BLAST FOR ME I & II

ROTTEN TO THE CORE I II III

A BRONX TALE I, II, III

DUFFLE BAG CARTEL I II III IV V VI

HEARTLESS GOON I II III IV V

A SAVAGE DOPEBOY I II

DRUG LORDS I II III

CUTTHROAT MAFIA I II

KING OF THE TRENCHES

By **Ghost**

LAY IT DOWN **I & II**

LAST OF A DYING BREED I II

BLOOD STAINS OF A SHOTTA I & II III

By **Jamaica**

LOYAL TO THE GAME I II III

LIFE OF SIN I, II III

By **TJ & Jelissa**

BLOODY COMMAS I & II

SKI MASK CARTEL I II & III

KING OF NEW YORK I II,III IV V

RISE TO POWER I II III

COKE KINGS I II III IV V

BORN HEARTLESS I II III IV

KING OF THE TRAP I II

By **T.J. Edwards**

IF LOVING HIM IS WRONG…I & II

LOVE ME EVEN WHEN IT HURTS I II III

By **Jelissa**

WHEN THE STREETS CLAP BACK I & II III

THE HEART OF A SAVAGE I II III

MONEY MAFIA

LOYAL TO THE SOIL

By **Jibril Williams**

A DISTINGUISHED THUG STOLE MY HEART I II & III

LOVE SHOULDN'T HURT I II III IV

RENEGADE BOYS I II III IV

PAID IN KARMA I II III

SAVAGE STORMS I II

AN UNFORESEEN LOVE I II

By **Meesha**

A GANGSTER'S CODE I &, II III

A GANGSTER'S SYN I II III

THE SAVAGE LIFE I II III

CHAINED TO THE STREETS I II III

BLOOD ON THE MONEY I II III

A GANGSTA'S PAIN

By **J-Blunt**

PUSH IT TO THE LIMIT

By **Bre' Hayes**

BLOOD OF A BOSS **I, II, III, IV, V**

SHADOWS OF THE GAME

TRAP BASTARD

By **Askari**

THE STREETS BLEED MURDER **I, II & III**

THE HEART OF A GANGSTA I II& III

Romell Tukes

By **Jerry Jackson**

CUM FOR ME I II III IV V VI VII

An **LDP Erotica Collaboration**

BRIDE OF A HUSTLA **I II & II**

THE FETTI GIRLS **I, II& III**

CORRUPTED BY A GANGSTA I, II III, IV

BLINDED BY HIS LOVE

THE PRICE YOU PAY FOR LOVE I, II ,III

DOPE GIRL MAGIC I II III

By **Destiny Skai**

WHEN A GOOD GIRL GOES BAD

By **Adrienne**

THE COST OF LOYALTY I II III

By Kweli

A GANGSTER'S REVENGE **I II III & IV**

THE BOSS MAN'S DAUGHTERS I II III IV V

A SAVAGE LOVE **I & II**

BAE BELONGS TO ME I II

A HUSTLER'S DECEIT I, II, III

WHAT BAD BITCHES DO I, II, III

SOUL OF A MONSTER I II III

KILL ZONE

A DOPE BOY'S QUEEN I II III

By **Aryanna**

A KINGPIN'S AMBITON

A KINGPIN'S AMBITION **II**

I MURDER FOR THE DOUGH

A Dopeboy's Dream 3

By **Ambitious**

TRUE SAVAGE I II III IV V VI VII

DOPE BOY MAGIC I, II, III

MIDNIGHT CARTEL I II III

CITY OF KINGZ I II

NIGHTMARE ON SILENT AVE

By **Chris Green**

A DOPEBOY'S PRAYER

By **Eddie "Wolf" Lee**

THE KING CARTEL **I, II & III**

By **Frank Gresham**

THESE NIGGAS AIN'T LOYAL **I, II & III**

By **Nikki Tee**

GANGSTA SHYT **I II &III**

By **CATO**

THE ULTIMATE BETRAYAL

By **Phoenix**

BOSS'N UP **I , II & III**

By **Royal Nicole**

I LOVE YOU TO DEATH

By **Destiny J**

I RIDE FOR MY HITTA

I STILL RIDE FOR MY HITTA

By **Misty Holt**

LOVE & CHASIN' PAPER

By **Qay Crockett**

TO DIE IN VAIN

Romell Tukes

SINS OF A HUSTLA
By **ASAD**
BROOKLYN HUSTLAZ
By **Boogsy Morina**
BROOKLYN ON LOCK I & II
By **Sonovia**
GANGSTA CITY
By **Teddy Duke**
A DRUG KING AND HIS DIAMOND I & II III
A DOPEMAN'S RICHES
HER MAN, MINE'S TOO I, II
CASH MONEY HO'S
THE WIFEY I USED TO BE I II
By Nicole Goosby
TRAPHOUSE KING **I II & III**
KINGPIN KILLAZ I II III
STREET KINGS I II
PAID IN BLOOD **I II**
CARTEL KILLAZ I II III
DOPE GODS I II
By **Hood Rich**
LIPSTICK KILLAH **I, II, III**
CRIME OF PASSION I II & III
FRIEND OR FOE I II III
By **Mimi**
STEADY MOBBN' **I, II, III**
THE STREETS STAINED MY SOUL I II

A Dopeboy's Dream 3

By **Marcellus Allen**

WHO SHOT YA **I, II, III**

SON OF A DOPE FIEND I II

HEAVEN GOT A GHETTO

Renta

GORILLAZ IN THE BAY **I II III IV**

TEARS OF A GANGSTA I II

3X KRAZY I II

STRAIGHT BEAST MODE

DE'KARI

TRIGGADALE I II III

MURDAROBER WAS THE CASE

Elijah R. Freeman

GOD BLESS THE TRAPPERS I, II, III

THESE SCANDALOUS STREETS I, II, III

FEAR MY GANGSTA I, II, III IV, V

THESE STREETS DON'T LOVE NOBODY I, II

BURY ME A G I, II, III, IV, V

A GANGSTA'S EMPIRE I, II, III, IV

THE DOPEMAN'S BODYGAURD I II

THE REALEST KILLAZ I II III

THE LAST OF THE OGS I II III

Tranay Adams

THE STREETS ARE CALLING

Duquie Wilson

MARRIED TO A BOSS I II III

By Destiny Skai & Chris Green

KINGZ OF THE GAME I II III IV V VI

Playa Ray

SLAUGHTER GANG I II III

RUTHLESS HEART I II III

By Willie Slaughter

FUK SHYT

By Blakk Diamond

DON'T F#CK WITH MY HEART I II

By Linnea

ADDICTED TO THE DRAMA I II III

IN THE ARM OF HIS BOSS II

By Jamila

YAYO I II III IV

A SHOOTER'S AMBITION I II

BRED IN THE GAME

By S. Allen

TRAP GOD I II III

RICH $AVAGE

MONEY IN THE GRAVE I II

By Martell Troublesome Bolden

FOREVER GANGSTA

GLOCKS ON SATIN SHEETS I II

By Adrian Dulan

TOE TAGZ I II III

LEVELS TO THIS SHYT I II

By Ah'Million

KINGPIN DREAMS I II III

A Dopeboy's Dream 3

By Paper Boi Rari

CONFESSIONS OF A GANGSTA I II III IV

By Nicholas Lock

I'M NOTHING WITHOUT HIS LOVE

SINS OF A THUG

TO THE THUG I LOVED BEFORE

By Monet Dragun

CAUGHT UP IN THE LIFE I II III

THE STREETS NEVER LET GO

By Robert Baptiste

NEW TO THE GAME I II III

MONEY, MURDER & MEMORIES I II III

By Malik D. Rice

LIFE OF A SAVAGE I II III

A GANGSTA'S QUR'AN I II III

MURDA SEASON I II III

GANGLAND CARTEL I II III

CHI'RAQ GANGSTAS I II III

KILLERS ON ELM STREET I II III

JACK BOYZ N DA BRONX I II III

A DOPEBOY'S DREAM I II III

By Romell Tukes

LOYALTY AIN'T PROMISED I II

By Keith Williams

QUIET MONEY I II III

THUG LIFE I II III

EXTENDED CLIP I II

Romell Tukes

By **Trai'Quan**
THE STREETS MADE ME I II III
By **Larry D. Wright**
THE ULTIMATE SACRIFICE I, II, III, IV, V, VI
KHADIFI
IF YOU CROSS ME ONCE
ANGEL I II
IN THE BLINK OF AN EYE
By **Anthony Fields**
THE LIFE OF A HOOD STAR
By **Ca$h & Rashia Wilson**
THE STREETS WILL NEVER CLOSE
By **K'ajji**
CREAM I II
By **Yolanda Moore**
NIGHTMARES OF A HUSTLA I II III
By **King Dream**
CONCRETE KILLA I II
VICIOUS LOYALTY
By **Kingpen**
HARD AND RUTHLESS I II
MOB TOWN 251
THE BILLIONAIRE BENTLEYS
By **Von Diesel**
GHOST MOB
Stilloan Robinson
MOB TIES I II III IV

A Dopeboy's Dream 3

By SayNoMore

BODYMORE MURDERLAND I II III

By Delmont Player

FOR THE LOVE OF A BOSS

By C. D. Blue

MOBBED UP I II III IV

THE BRICK MAN I II

By King Rio

KILLA KOUNTY

By Khufu

MONEY GAME I II

By Smoove Dolla

A GANGSTA'S KARMA

By FLAME

KING OF THE TRENCHES II

by **GHOST & TRANAY ADAMS**

QUEEN OF THE ZOO

By **Black Migo**

BOOKS BY LDP'S CEO, CA$H

TRUST IN NO MAN

TRUST IN NO MAN 2

TRUST IN NO MAN 3

BONDED BY BLOOD

SHORTY GOT A THUG

THUGS CRY

THUGS CRY 2

THUGS CRY 3

TRUST NO BITCH

TRUST NO BITCH 2

TRUST NO BITCH 3

TIL MY CASKET DROPS

RESTRAINING ORDER

RESTRAINING ORDER 2

IN LOVE WITH A CONVICT

LIFE OF A HOOD STAR

A Dopeboy's Dream 3